The characters and events portrayed in this book are fictitious. Any similarity to real persons, living or dead, is coincidental and not intended by the author. Any reference to real locations is only for atmospheric effect, and in no way truly represents those locations. Any opinions on businesses or real locations or anything of the sort are merely the fictitious opinions of the viewpoint character, and in no way reflect the author's opinions, or bear any truth—they are purely for immersive effect.

Copyright © 2025 by Ryan Casey

Cover design by Miblart

All rights reserved.

No part of this book may be reproduced in any form or by any electronic or mechanical means, including information storage and retrieval systems, without written permission from the author, except for the use of brief quotations in a book review.

Published by Higher Bank Books

PANDEMIC Z 8: BREAKDOWN

A Post Apocalyptic Zombie Thriller

PANDEMIC Z
BOOK 8

RYAN CASEY

GET A POST APOCALYPTIC NOVEL FOR FREE

To instantly receive an exclusive post apocalyptic novel totally free, sign up for Ryan Casey's author newsletter at: ryancaseybooks.com/fanclub

CHAPTER ONE

1967

Walter Henshaw paced down the corridor and tried to keep his shit together.

But it was pretty damned hard to keep your shit together when you'd been summoned down to the bunker.

He'd been here before. A number of times. It was the height of the Cold War, and experimentation was rife, so top-secret projects were in full flow. He should be used to this place by now. Used to coming down here, seeing what the nation's top scientists had been working on.

But this place never lost its creepiness.

It was dimly lit, for one. Aged concrete walls sweated with condensation. A hum of machinery buzzed away in the background. A distant echo of radio transmissions, filling the air.

It smelled of cigarette smoke. Walter didn't smoke. He was one of the few people who didn't. His friends all smoked. His beloved Joyce, she smoked like a chimney.

But he just didn't like it. He just couldn't take to it. He didn't like the sensation, as it caught the back of his throat. The bitterness in his mouth the following morning. The way it dulled the taste of his food. Which wasn't always such a terrible thing. He would never tell Joyce as much. But her cooking wasn't always the greatest. Seasoning. That was the issue. She never seasoned food. Or she criminally *under*-seasoned it, anyway.

He'd never tell Joyce that, though. He loved her dearly. Loved her ever since he first laid eyes on her, twenty years ago. Right after the war. The glory days. The golden years. Seeing her in that bar, staring over at him with those gorgeous chocolate-brown eyes. She was his love. She was his forever.

And if that meant eating her damned under-seasoned pork every once in a while, then that's sure as hell exactly what he'd do.

There was another smell in the air, as he made his way further down this endless corridor. Something sterile. Antiseptic. In itself, it wasn't such a bad smell. It was fresh enough.

But the fact that it was clearly there to mask something else was the problem.

That made it so, so much worse by association.

He walked down this corridor with a military officer just ahead of him and adjusted his tie. It was a little too tight around his throat. Made it hard to breathe. Joyce had bought it him for Christmas. *You need a real fancy tie after your promotion,* she said. She was proud of him. So damned proud.

Which was funny since he couldn't even tell her—his own wife —exactly what it was he did.

He didn't find it hard to keep what he did confidential. He didn't like talking about work. Work was the most boring damned thing to talk about, in his opinion. And yet, it was all anyone ever seemed to want to talk about.

He never understood it. He couldn't think of a time when he was genuinely interested in hearing about someone else's job. About what was going on at their workplace. He timed out. Glazed over. Maybe that was a reflection of his character, but he wasn't sure.

Perhaps it was because he had one of the more interesting jobs imaginable, and everything else paled in comparison.

Maybe it was the frustration of not being able to talk about his job, equalising the conversation somewhat.

He looked over his shoulder. Back up the corridor. It stretched on for miles. These tunnels, weaving underground. You assume when you're standing on the floor in your kitchen that there's nothing under there. Soil, pipes, earth. You couldn't be more wrong. There's a whole world under your feet. A whole hidden world.

Unthinkable things, going on right beneath you.

He wasn't sure how long he was walking before they finally stopped at the door in question. The guard stood beside him. Looked right at him with wide eyes. He looked at him with a sort of jealousy. A kind of envy. Because this was the end of the road for him. He couldn't go any further. He was forbidden from seeing what secrets awaited behind these doors.

That's just how it had to be.

He stepped up to the camera. Stood in front of it. Felt unknown digital things going on—scanning his eye, shit he didn't understand. He was a government official. Head of the O.R.I.O.N Project.

He couldn't even tell people what that acronym stood for.

Sometimes, he had to pinch himself.

Observation and Research into Interstellar Organisms and Nanotechnology.

It began in 1965. A top-secret Cold War initiative, aimed at developing advanced human augmentation using a mysterious substance found in a meteorite. The goal? Simple. Creating superior soldiers. Stronger. Faster. Resistant to biowarfare. Giving the United States and its allies an edge in global conflicts.

The O.R.I.O.N Project wasn't just limited to the States. Britain and France were involved. The Soviets were undoubtedly undergoing their own research. They had launched their own space programs. And they were finding things. Discovering things. Things that could give nations an edge. Control space, control her strength, and you can learn how to control the planet.

Initially, it was a case of throwing everything against a wall and seeing whether it stuck or not. Testing unusual discoveries on mice, rats, and chimps.

There was limited progress, originally. Signs that things from outer space *could* contribute to change. Not always positive change, either.

That was until they found the substance.

The one they coined Vesperium.

Scientists found it in a meteorite. This black, treacle-like substance. Strangely fluid—one moment, liquid, the next, a fungal-like growth. And sometimes, small and bug-like. Capable of changing its form in an instant.

They tested it on the mice.

They tested it on the rats.

They tested it on the chimps.

And they saw it.

They saw it for themselves.

What it could do.

What it was capable of.

He'd seen enough to suggest that it was worth a human trial. The things he'd seen. The transformations in the animals.

Heightened reflexes.

Increased strength.

Rapid healing.

He'd never forget walking through these thick metal doors just three weeks ago.

Inside, men in white lab coats standing there, rigidly. Whispering.

A containment chamber, right there in the middle—a thick glass cell, harshly lit, with a single *subject* sitting inside.

A volunteer.

Although that wasn't true, was it?

They were a prisoner. Death row prisoner. Given a second chance at life.

Sitting there, shirtless, on a metal chair.

IV in their arm.

Connected to a bag filled with a thick, black fluid.

The Treatment.

Vesperium.

Walter would never forget what he asked. "And you're sure it's safe?"

The lead scientist—Callum Fischer—paused. Glanced at the subject. "It's... reacting. Exactly as we witnessed in the animals."

Walter watched. The subject started breathing, deeply. Smiling. Clenching and unclenching their fists. "I feel... strong," they whispered.

Then, out of nowhere, Walter couldn't really describe it, but a strange humming noise filled the room.

Not from the equipment.

From...

Inside the subject.

And then the subject started writhing around.

Arching their back.

Veins pulsating on their neck.

Blood spurting out of their lips.

Screaming.

Shaking.

Crying.

This aggression. This pure state of aggression, as the lights flickered.

That was all Walter needed to see.

A sign.

A sign that they were on to something here.

That they could harness this.

If they could use this treatment—Vesperium—to heighten the

aggression, reflexes, and reactions of their troops, then America could rule the world.

And beyond.

There was something else from the animal trials, too.

Evidence that Vesperium created a kind of hive mind.

A kind of telepathy.

A *knowing* that went beyond their current understanding.

Tests that proceeded to more subjects. More subjects that he commissioned.

A way of harnessing that anger.

Balancing it.

A way of making it work *for* them.

Controlling it, like they were able to in the animal testing.

He couldn't stop thinking about it. He lay awake at night, the screams of the subject permeating his dreams.

Screams, and...

Something else.

A vision.

A vision of something in the sky.

Something descending to Earth.

Something getting...

Closer.

He didn't go down to the bunker again. He allowed the trials to unfold from a distance. While he was intrigued by progress, he couldn't deny that something else was there, too.

Something he could only feasibly describe as a *fear*.

He never went back.

Until now.

The metal doors shrieked open.

The sight was the same as last time, in some ways.

That glass inspection chamber, dominating this dimly lit room.

People in white coats, all surrounding this chamber.

Only...

There was something very different.

The humming noise.

Inside the subject.

Growing louder.

His skin was rippling.

His veins, pulsating, were black.

And his pupils—he thought of him as a *he* now, and not a "subject", because it was hard to maintain that self-delusion for too long—were dilating unnaturally.

Turning fully black.

Walter stood there.

In the middle of this room.

Staring at the subject.

"How long has this—"

"Thirty minutes," Callum Fischer said. He looked worried. And he smelled of sweat.

He looked around at the subject. The man. He was screaming. Writhing around. His fingers, curling unnaturally. That humming noise, ever louder. The lights above. Flickering away.

He wasn't sure how long this went on.

But suddenly, the subject stopped.

He arched his back.

Pushed his shoulders right back.

Mouth opening in a silent scream.

His bones seemed to crack.

And then...

Silence.

Walter stood there.

Callum stood with him.

The room silent, other than the beeps of the computers, and the whirring of the machinery.

"Is he..." Walter started.

And then, out of the subject's throat, a second voice.

It sounded *almost* human.

Almost.

But it had a distorted, inhuman frequency.

Like it was *inside* him.

Like it was *singing.*

Suddenly, the subject's flesh split open.

Right down the middle of his chest.

But there was no blood.

Only...

This writhing, chitinous black layer underneath.

Glistening.

Glistening like something *unfinished.*

The room shook.

And Walter could only stand there.

Walter could only stare, as this *new form* burst its way out of the man's body underneath.

He stumbled backwards, as it cracked against the solid glass.

As the room shook.

As lights flickered brighter.

"Contain the subject!" someone shouted.

But then the bunker's radio equipment screeched with interference, drowning out those cries.

Callum grabbed Walter's arm, then. Tight. He looked at him with these wide, fascinated eyes. Terrified. But fascinated. Like Doctor Frankenstein, witnessing the awakening of his monster.

"Sir," he said. "We've done it."

We've done it? Done *what?*

"We've... we've sent the signal," he said. "It knows we're here."

That was the part that Walter had left out.

The *second* part of these investigations.

The new layer that the O.R.I.O.N Project had reached.

The communication.

Because the more tests they did, the more they began to realise that not only was the Treatment enhancing them...

It was *rewriting* them.

And the more people were exposed... the more they detected *signals*.

Strange signals from above.

Signs.

Signs that something was out there.

That something in deep space was *listening*.

"We've sent the signal," Callum repeated. "It knows... it knows we're here."

A deep, reverberating noise rolled through the bunker.

Not an explosion.

A *response*.

Just like the sound that came out of the subject's mouth, before this *being* broke out of his body.

They did not know it yet, right there in that lab in 1967.

But the O.R.I.O.N Project had just unknowingly triggered a summoning event.

The beginning of an "infection" that would take decades to unfold.

Fifty-seven years, to be precise.

And when it did unfold... nothing was going to be the same.

Ever again.

CHAPTER TWO

Brian tilted his head up towards the sky.
But nothing could prepare him for what he was about to see.

He was crouched in the entrance area to Galloway's supposed "safe zone." It was pitch black. Late. He was wearing his muddy jeans, and a shirt, which was ripped and covered in blood. He could taste blood, too. His head ached, and his jaw hurt. His ears were ringing. Really loudly. By all accounts, he felt like shit. Total shit.

But it was hard to feel *completely* shit.

Because Abigail was here.

She was right beside him. In his arms. Holding on to him. His daughter. He'd searched so far for her. Spent so long trying to track her down. Some days, he lost hope. Hope of ever finding her again. Some days—the especially hard days—he suspected that she might be dead. Because why should she be alive? Why should she have survived when so many others hadn't? What made her any different? What made her special?

But for the most part, he had maintained his hope. There was a sense, in the back of his mind, that he would see her again, and that all their differences would disappear in a moment. Far-fetched, maybe. But something he dreamed of.

That moment was here.

Right now.

She was here. In his arms.

Only...

It wasn't as simple as that.

Georgia was here, too. Georgia, who he had spent so long traversing the country with in search of safety, all that time ago. Which was mad. Absolutely mad. Finding Abigail. That was crazy in itself. She looked tired. Pale. Weak.

But finding *Georgia* here, too.

And, by the looks of things, in an even worse state.

Even thinner.

Even paler.

But *here*.

All roads led to Galloway, it seemed.

The dogs were here, too. They were currently gathering around the twitching body of this man. The guard. The one who'd kicked the shit out of Brian on the way down here.

He was dead, now.

But so too was another woman.

Someone Georgia had called "Grace."

She'd fallen into Georgia's arms after being shot. After taking a bullet. Georgia was still holding her. She was definitely dead, though. Bled out, by the looks of things.

And Brian saw mixed emotions in Georgia's eyes.

He saw anger.

He saw sadness.

He saw confusion.

He wanted to hold Abigail, the dogs, and Georgia, and he wanted to savour this moment. He wanted it to last forever. The way it felt.

Because this reunion was everything he'd worked towards.

This was everything he'd wanted.

But...

He couldn't shake what he'd just witnessed from his mind.

Galloway.

Stepping out, on that balcony, in the distance.

Standing there, over the entrance area of this safe zone.

And *looking up* at something.

Looking up. Just like the infected had looked up, on the road, when Brian should have met his maker.

Brian had watched Galloway. Staring up at the sky. He'd seen his smile widening. And also the fear in his eyes.

Like he was making a discovery.

A terrifying discovery.

"It was right," he'd said. "It was all right. The O.R.I.O.N Project. What it warned of. All of it."

And then he'd looked back down at Brian.

Right into *his* eyes.

"Don't look up," he'd said.

And then...

He'd started drifting *upwards*.

Towards the sky.

Brian knew he had to be tripping. The substance. That parasitic mould. It had to be that. Fucking with his mind. Or maybe the infected. Maybe they were close. Their proximity, messing with his perception.

But...

Watching Galloway rise.

Watching him climb towards the sky.

He had this deep sense that this wasn't in his head.

That this was *real*.

He watched him rise.

And in the corner of his eyes, he swore he saw *more* people rising.

People climbing upwards.

Climbing right towards the sky, and...
And that's when it struck him that this had to be a dream.
Because...
Emma.
Emma. The girl he'd met at the start of everything. She'd gone missing. Really early on.
But now she was here, too.
She was here.
And she was pregnant.
And something was wrong.
Something was very wrong.
Alarm sirens rang out all around this place.
Gunshots.
Firing.
Shouting.
Shrieking.
Screaming.
And all Brian could do was lift his head.
All he could do was follow Galloway, as he rose towards the sky.
All he could do was the exact opposite of what Galloway told him.
"*Don't look up.*"
He couldn't stop himself.
Curiosity.
Curiosity, taking hold, and...
A hand.
Wrapping around his arm.
Squeezing it.
Tight.
A voice.
A soft voice.
A gentle voice.
A shaky voice.

"Don't look up," it whispered.

And it was the only voice that could stop him.

It was the only voice that could stop him from looking up.

The only voice that could make him freeze, right there.

Freeze, and stop following Galloway, as he rose towards the sky.

He got the sense that there was something up there.

There was something above.

Something he needed to look at.

Something he *needed* to see.

And that voice—Abigail's voice, his daughter's voice—was the only thing stopping him right now.

"Don't look up," she repeated. "Or..."

But then, something else.

An *urge*.

The only way he could put it.

This urge.

Making him fight against Abigail's wishes.

Making him want to keep following Galloway.

Want to keep looking.

"Don't look up, Dad," Abigail said. Squeezing his arm tighter. The screams around them getting louder. And in the corners of his eyes, more people. Rising up. Rising to the sky above.

"Don't do it. Don't..."

He wanted to fight against this instinct.

He wanted to listen to his daughter.

He wanted to break free of this trance.

But nothing could stop what happened next.

He swallowed a lump in his throat.

He closed his burning eyes.

He tilted his head right back.

And then, he opened his eyes.

He looked up.

CHAPTER THREE

Ava opened her eyes, and she knew she was in danger right away when she heard the loud alarms ringing out.

And the screams.

They were coming from outside. But she didn't know where *inside* was. She didn't know where she was. It was so dark. Pitch black.

Only...

There was a little red light. Flashing, on and off. Not fast. Just glowing on, and then off, and on, and off again. It seemed to be something to do with the alarm. This weird, noisy alarm, that sounded like when they had fire alarm tests at school, and they all had to go outside and line up. Except that one time when David Barton hit the alarm, and the fire brigade came, and they got everyone to sit down on benches, which were usually just for the older kids in Year 6, which made her realise just how serious it all was.

She knew David Barton had hit the alarm. She'd seen it happen. He was a bad kid. She wanted to tell on him.

But she didn't.

For some reason, she kept his secret. Even though he was

never nice to her. She didn't want to get him in trouble. She worried he might do something horrible to her in revenge.

And maybe by not grassing on him, he'd start to be nicer to her. He wouldn't bully her. Because she knew who'd hit the alarm. And she could just tell on him if ever he was mean to her.

But it didn't last long.

He was walking past her in the corridor one day, and he spat in her face, then put chewing gum in her hair.

She was so annoyed that she went over to the fire alarm.

She smashed it.

Then she went straight to the teacher and told her that David Barton had done it.

That time, she didn't care.

This alarm was different, though. It sounded *higher*.

And there was another noise, too.

A weird noise.

Like…

Something was *humming*.

Humming so loud that she could *feel* it in her chest.

She blinked a few times. Her eyes were sore. Her head was aching. Really badly. For some reason, she couldn't remember where she was. How she'd ended up here. When she tried to remember, it just sort of slipped between her fingers. Like when she was getting closer to a rainbow. It just drifted, further and further away…

And then she heard something.

It sounded… wet. Like wet footsteps. It sounded… familiar, weirdly. There was something about it that *felt* familiar. Almost like when Mum came into her bedroom when she was sleeping, and creaked across the floor, and sat on the edge of her bed and just watched her sleep. It kind of felt like that now.

She blinked a few times. Mum. She couldn't remember. But for some reason, she felt like something had happened to Mum. Where was Mum? What was…

It came back to her, then.

All of it, in a rush.

Finding Brian.

Galloway taking her.

Keeping her in the restaurant.

Then...

Then, showing her *Mum*.

Telling her about these weird things he'd found—things from space, something called ORION, and how it was going to make humanity better, and all this stuff she didn't understand, and...

And then she'd got out of the restaurant, and she'd gone to the place Galloway had taken her to, the place where Mum was, deep underground, and she'd tried to kill Mum, because Mum wasn't Mum anymore; Mum was hurt, and she was suffering, and...

And then something had happened.

She'd walked over to that computer.

She'd pushed a button.

She didn't know what it was.

And she didn't know why she was pushing it.

But when she pushed it...

The lights went out.

A siren started ringing.

And...

Footsteps.

Wet footsteps.

Right beside her.

She turned around. Slowly. Lying on the floor, for some reason. Heart beating really fast. A weird taste in her mouth. A taste that reminded her of sick.

She could hear something. Right at the other side of the table that Mum was on.

Only...

She looked up at that metal table.

When the light shone bright, she noticed something.

Mum wasn't there anymore.

This black stuff was there.

Mushrooms were rolling off the side of it.

Steam coming out of them.

And she saw something else, too.

Something at the other side of the table.

Standing there.

It was standing really still. She couldn't see it properly. She only had a couple of seconds to see it. When that red light flashed on.

When she saw it, though, she realised it looked a bit like Mum.

It was Mum.

Standing there.

Only...

It went dark again.

But just before it did, she saw Mum turning around.

Looking towards her.

She held her breath.

Her heart beat even faster.

That alarm, getting louder. While outside somewhere, she swore she could hear screaming. Gunshots.

She waited for the room to light up again. It felt like forever.

Sitting there.

Crouched.

Right beside the table.

She held her breath, as that red light started to shine again.

And this time...

She saw her.

Mum *was* standing there.

She was looking down at her.

Right at her.

Her long hair was dangling down onto her shoulders. It looked really greasy. And there was a weird, nasty smell, too. Which must be coming from Mum.

She was naked. Which was weird to see. She'd walked in on Mum naked a couple of times, and it always made her really embarrassed.

But now… it didn't even seem like it *was* Mum.

She was covered in this stuff. Stuff that Ava thought was blood at first.

But when she looked closer at it, she realised it was dark.

Black.

Goo.

And…

Mum's eyes.

Looking right at her.

There was something weird about them.

They *weren't* Mum's eyes at all.

They looked…

Empty.

Like deep, black wells.

And they were moving, too.

Moving slightly.

Like…

Like they were trying to figure out exactly where eyes should go.

Like they were looking right at her, and trying to figure it out.

And that's when Ava realised the rest of Mum's body started doing that, too.

Her face. Flickering.

Changing.

Eyes blinking weirdly.

Mouth moving. As if she was talking. But no sounds were coming out.

And it looked like she was walking towards her.

Like she was stepping towards her.

But she didn't move.

She stepped, but she was still in the same spot.

Ava looked up at her, as the light started to darken again.

She saw her opening her mouth.

And there was a *sound* coming from her mouth.

A weird sound.

An *almost* sound.

Like a conversation that never happened.

Or like she was calling her name, but like it was being played backwards.

She was just...

Wrong.

She watched the red light fade.

She held her breath more.

She waited for Mum to appear again.

And then the red light illuminated the room.

When it did, Ava wished it hadn't.

CHAPTER FOUR

Georgia held Grace in her arms and tried to wrap her head around everything she was witnessing.

But it was impossible.

There was just too much to process.

And they were still in danger.

Grave danger.

She held Grace in her arms. Grace had gone quiet. And still, too. There was something distinctly different about a lifeless body. When someone is just sleeping or unconscious, the body holds itself in a different way to when it's dead. Must be some sort of internal muscle memory.

But when someone is dead... that is different. Very different. She'd seen it before. Her aunt. When she was younger. On that rollercoaster with her. Climbing up to the top of the slope. The wind in her hair. The nerves in her tummy, swirling around, as she got closer to the top.

Then Auntie Winnie leaning on her shoulder.

She thought she was just resting her head on her shoulder at first. Lying on her. Scared.

But there was something different about the way she *felt*.

It was like her body was jelly.

Like there was no strength in it at all.

She'd had a heart attack, apparently. But she still rode the whole rollercoaster. Georgia had to ride that coaster with her dead body.

In a way, she told herself that Auntie Winnie had died doing something she loved most. That made her feel a bit better about it. But looking back, she figured it was a rather traumatic experience for her. Entirely abnormal thing to go through. You don't really realise that at the time, though, especially as a kid, do you?

On the other hand, she realised what she was experiencing right now was entirely abnormal.

She held Grace in her arms.

In front of her, that man. The one who had shot her. The prick who had put a bullet through her. Killed her.

Grace had stepped in front of that bullet.

And now she was gone.

She'd looked Georgia in the eye, and she'd told her she was sorry—for the betrayal, for everything—and then she'd taken that bullet.

And she'd done something else, too.

Her kids.

Her children.

Theo.

Elizabeth.

She'd told her to get to them.

To help them.

And even though Georgia couldn't envision *ever* wanting to help a woman who had betrayed her, and then let people suffer the greatest miseries, all for her own selfish desires... she was doing it for her children.

And while Georgia didn't have children of her own, she could understand it. The things a parent would do for the ones they loved.

And in the end... in the end, she'd chosen to help Georgia. She'd helped her and Abigail out of that room they were tied up in, after their failed escape attempt. And then she'd thrown herself in front of a bullet.

She'd sacrificed herself.

She'd done everything for her children.

But she'd also taken a bullet for someone she didn't know.

And now she was dead.

Georgia wished she had the time to process that.

But she didn't.

At all.

Because there were other things to process, too.

Abigail. And her dad. Brian. Appearing. Out of nowhere. Beaten. Bruised.

But here.

Alive.

Just as she'd suspected all along.

She felt this elation when she saw Brian. She'd connected with him. Deeply. Their journey up north, to the fallen safe haven, all that time ago. They'd truly connected. Truly bonded.

And maybe that was partly why she'd never lost hope. Why she'd always believed he was still out there, somewhere. That, and the fact there was no trace of him in that cellar. And she was convinced there had to be.

She looked at him, the dogs, and his daughter, as she stood there with Grace, and she saw someone else.

A woman. One Brian seemed to recognise.

Which was... unusual.

Because she looked *odd*.

It was hard to explain. Something just wasn't right with her. Her skin. It was pale. So pale that it was almost translucent.

And her eyes.

They didn't seem to connect with anyone.

They seemed to... *shift,* almost.

And she was pregnant, too.

Heavily pregnant.

Barefoot.

Holding her pregnant belly.

And even despite this array of sensory chaos, that still wasn't everything.

The screaming.

Behind her.

The gunshots.

The sirens, ringing.

Alarms.

The lights.

Shining brightly one second.

Gone the next.

She stood there, still in disbelief at everything that was unfolding. From spending so long in captivity, to *this*...

It didn't seem real.

But it was.

She looked over at Brian.

He was lifting his head.

Lifting his head, as if there was something above him.

Something up there.

And Georgia didn't want to look up.

Because she'd heard that Galloway cunt telling people not to look up, and then...

She'd hardly had time to process anything.

She could only stand there.

Holding Grace.

Listening to the screams.

Looking at the fear in the eyes of those immediately around her.

She watched Brian, as he held on to his daughter.

She watched him, the dogs surrounding him, almost in a protective bubble.

She watched him, as he tilted his head, higher, and higher, and higher.

She watched as his eyes settled on something above.

She watched them widen.

She saw the amazement.

She saw the fear.

And then, right there, in front of her... Georgia witnessed something unlike anything she had ever seen before.

CHAPTER FIVE

Galloway's first name was Curtis.

He never liked his name. Kids used to bully him for it at school. He wasn't entirely sure why. It wasn't like it was an especially weird name or anything. There were definitely weirder names in school. But for some reason, it stuck. *Dirty Curty*. Stuff like that. Silly stuff. Stuff that, looking back, shouldn't really have hurt him. It wouldn't hurt him now. So there was no reason why it should have hurt him then.

But it did. Because they picked on him for anything, really. And if it wasn't Curtis they took the mickey out of, it would be something else.

That's something he'd realised, as he got older. In primary school, Curtis was just something easy for them to poke fun at. Basically, they'd smelled blood from the off. And that's what it came down to. He showed difference. In the school world, much like the animal kingdom, difference meant weakness. It could've been his name. It could've been the way he walked. It could've been *anything*. His name was just an easy thing to latch on to.

When he reached high school, he took a different approach.

He decided to suppress all of his weirdness. He decided to suppress most of everything. He remained quiet. He didn't express strong opinions on anything at all—other than things that would quite obviously not cause any controversy. He remained stoic. And although it did see him called a "weirdo" by a few of his peers, it was better than being bullied relentlessly.

But strangely, he never truly shook off that self-consciousness about his entirely normal name.

So he went through several different first names.

And in the end, he just settled on "Galloway."

He liked that. It had something of a ring to it. It sounded authoritative. Which was exactly what he needed now he was a leader.

He'd very accidentally fallen into leadership. He'd never seen himself as a leader. But strangely enough, people came to him for advice. He'd asked a girl about it once. She said it was that strong, silent demeanour. It gave off an aura of confidence. Of self-assuredness. It made people come to him for advice. It made people follow his judgement.

And it taught him that life was better when you said less.

When you repressed opinions.

And when you kept things to yourself.

He remembered the discovery he'd made. Underground. The labs. The old, ancient labs.

He remembered dusting off those documents.

Reading through them.

The shit about some old Cold War project.

The O.R.I.O.N Project.

Testing. Testing on minerals from space.

Minerals that *strengthened* people.

That *rewrote* them somehow.

He didn't know what he was reading. He couldn't make sense of it. It had to be bollocks. Total, sci-fi bollocks.

But...

The infection.

The outbreak.

The things he'd witnessed.

The stuff about heightened aggression.

And then about the *second* form.

Even the stuff about dogs counteracting the infection, somehow.

It added up.

It all added up.

And yet, these discoveries he made were deep, deep underground.

And they were discoveries written years ago, too.

Decades ago.

He thought about the discoveries he'd made, in a momentary flash.

He thought about the tests he'd done.

He thought about the research.

The things he'd found.

The stuff about the studies.

These tests. How wrong they'd gone. How they'd been shelved.

Because the researchers on the O.R.I.O.N project realised they weren't just studying this "Vesperium."

They were *being* studied, too.

The infection.

Its purpose.

Humanity had it wrong.

Everyone had it wrong.

They thought its goal was purely to spread.

To infect more people.

But that wasn't all.

The more it spread, the closer *it* got.

The more people the infection reached, the stronger the *signal* grew.

And when it reached a critical mass...

Something comes through.

And that's what Galloway wanted to discover.

The Threshold Event.

Part of him wanted to stop it from happening.

Part of him wanted to stop anything like that from spreading across Earth.

But at the same time... another part of him *wanted* to see it.

He wanted to bring it here.

He wanted to be the one that helped draw it closer.

He wanted to be a part of something new.

He knew, right now, that moment was finally here.

The moment he had been waiting for.

The moment *everything* was building towards.

He was rising.

Rising upwards.

Like he was being lifted by something.

Like gravity itself was failing him.

The world around him was distorting.

Reality itself, *warping,* as if to accommodate something.

He could see things moving in ways they shouldn't. The sky itself. Breaking into pieces. Shifting. Right before him.

And sometimes, he thought he saw things. Solid, concrete things. In a moment of pure anxiety, he understood. He understood completely.

And then, as soon as he'd seen these things, they slipped away again. From his mind. Out of his consciousness. They lost meaning. Lost all meaning. He forgot them, just as quickly as he'd seen them.

But he knew they'd terrified him. The things he'd seen.

He knew they'd peeled all the layers back, and made him feel fear.

A pure sense of fear.
Like a kidnapped child.
Defenceless.
He looked up, as he rose above, and as a bitterness filled his mouth.
The things he'd read.
The stages.
The three stages.
The Incubation Phase.
The Metamorphosis Phase.
The Threshold Event.
Dormancy.
Emergence.
Convergence.
Chrysalis.
Aberration.
Apotheosis.
He thought about those words.
He thought about all the mysteries.
The first two phases.
The detail in which they had been studied.
And then the third phase.
The final phase.
The one beginning right now.
What did that mean?
What happened now?
He held his breath.
He floated higher.
He felt his face burning, as light surrounded him.
His skin splitting.
His bones vibrating.
As it filled his body.
As it seeped through his skin, and into his flesh, and even into his bones.

He looked up at it.

He smiled even wider.

"I am your conduit," he said. "I hear your message. I..."

And then, everything went bright.

And Galloway felt himself falling away from Earth.

CHAPTER SIX

Brian didn't believe in aliens.
It wasn't that he didn't appreciate the logic. Because, sure. If life could exist on Earth, then why couldn't it exist elsewhere?

It was more the little grey man thing he didn't believe in. Because of the many myriad forms an "alien" could possibly take, why would they end up looking just like humans, just slightly... different?

Why would they have two eyes?

Why would they need two eyes at all?

Who was to say they even *looked* a way that anyone on Earth could even comprehend?

Maybe they didn't look like anything at all.

Maybe they didn't even *need* to see.

Maybe they had another sense that we couldn't even comprehend that rendered *seeing* worthless.

Maybe they didn't even *need* senses at all.

Maybe they just *were*.

Maybe they didn't even need to *be*.

You get the idea.

And the whole idea they cruised around on spaceships, too. It was an entirely narcissistic human thing to assume that in the entirety of the universe, extraterrestrial life was... decidedly human.

Almost like *we* were the pinnacle for other beings to base themselves on. The benchmark, as it were.

So it wasn't to say that Brian didn't believe in extraterrestrial life of some form. It seemed both impossible and also rather tragic that they might be alone in this universe. Or that they might be the pinnacle of evolution.

But the little grey men. Yeah. They were the ones Brian took issue with. They were the ones he didn't believe in, so much.

Also, how equally narcissistic to assume that some alien life forms out there would find Earth so interesting, purely because humans were interesting? Who was to say humans were interesting at all? Hell, Brian didn't even find most humans interesting.

So he didn't believe in aliens. Not the kind that humanity had invented, anyway.

But as he looked up into the sky right now... for the first time in his life, he began to question whether what he was witnessing could possibly have extraterrestrial origins.

It was in his head. It had to be in his head. That was his first thought. What he was seeing. What he was witnessing. It was in his imagination. It was all in his imagination.

Because what he was seeing wasn't real.

What he was seeing *couldn't* be real.

The sky. The dark sky above. It looked like it was *splitting*. Almost like it was peeling itself apart. Cracking open. His only frame of reference was that it felt like he was on the inside of an Easter egg, and someone had just split it open. And that there was something on the other side of it.

Something trying to break through.

The air itself felt like it was pressing down on him. Pushing down on the top of his head. And his shoulders. And right the way down his body. Like it was trying to squash him. He felt a sudden shift in temperature. A coldness, the likes of which he'd never felt before.

And he heard this hum, too.

A distant hum.

A strange frequency.

Growing louder, and yet still incomprehensible, somehow.

Almost as if it grew less comprehensible the louder it got.

Like a radio, dancing between tuned-in and white noise.

Shifting between channels.

He could see colours in the sky above. Purples, and blues, and the brightest yellows. Colours he'd never seen before, either. Ones he couldn't even properly recollect the moment they passed. And each and every different colour *felt* different somehow, too. He felt them. He felt them in his chest. In his entire body.

He was faintly aware of his daughter, right beside him. His daughter, Abigail, who he had spent so long trying to locate. So many months, hoping she was still out there. Losing hope sometimes. Wondering whether he might have lost her.

But she was here.

This should be the most momentous moment of his life.

But it was all overshadowed.

Everything was overshadowed.

By what was above.

By what he was looking at.

By what he was witnessing.

He remembered what Galloway had said.

"Don't look up."

Those words. As clear in his head now as the moment Galloway spoke them.

He wanted to follow his advice. He wanted to resist looking up.

But now he *was* looking up... there was nothing else he could do.

His amazement growing stronger.

His *fear*, building.

But not only fear.

Fear and excitement, too.

He watched the sky peel itself open.

He needed to see what was behind the darkness.

He needed to see the truth.

He needed to see it all, as gunshots fired all around him, and screams echoed around the place, and dogs barked, and people *rose* into the sky—literally rose, like they were on strings, and...

Emma.

He saw Emma.

It was strange.

It was as if she was in front of him, now.

Above him.

Looking down at him.

Only there was something different about her.

Something fundamentally different about her.

Something *off* about her.

Something that wasn't *Emma* about her.

He saw her in front of his vision.

Blocking his view of above.

He saw her, reaching towards him with those long, pale hands.

He saw her.

Then he saw the sky.

The colours.

And he felt it.

He felt burning in his face.

He felt that crushing sensation, pressing harder.

He felt his heart racing faster.

And every heartbeat hurting.

His body aching with the colours, and aching with the sounds and...

That's when he heard that word.

That one word.

Fear.

He heard that word, deep inside him—spoken from somewhere within—and at that moment, at that instant, he took a deep breath, and he let that fear pass through him.

He let it sit there.

He didn't try to fight it.

He didn't try to resist it.

He did nothing.

Just let it pass through him.

Let it wash over him.

Let it...

Fear is contagious.

He heard those words in his head again.

As if spoken by someone else.

He took a deep breath.

He swallowed a lump in his dry, sore throat.

And then he closed his eyes, and let the warmth take over him.

He didn't know how to explain what he'd just witnessed.

But little did he know, he would have even greater difficulty explaining what happened next.

CHAPTER SEVEN

Ava sometimes saw monsters at the foot of her bed in the middle of the night.

Back when the world was normal, anyway. Some nights, she would wake up, and she wouldn't be able to move. It was a bit like when Galloway had her in that restaurant, and he'd given her that medicine to stop her from moving. Only it was her whole body.

All she could do was lie there.

Heart racing.

Trying her hardest to move.

Every muscle in her body.

But she couldn't.

No matter how hard she tried.

And that was when she looked to the bottom of the bed, and she saw the monster.

It was always dark. Kind of like a person, hiding underneath a dark blanket. It didn't have any eyes. Not that she could see, anyway. Maybe it did have eyes. Really dark eyes, the same colour as the rest of its body.

But as she lay there in bed, unable to move a muscle, that monster wouldn't move. Not as long as *she* didn't try to move.

It would just sit there.

Watching her.

But when she got more scared, when she started trying...

It would hover over her.

Hover towards her.

Right towards her.

The monster never reached her. She would always be able to move before it did. She'd always wake up before it did.

But she worried what might happen if it *did* reach her one day.

For some reason, Ava was reminded of that sleep monster right now.

Mum usually came to comfort her when she'd seen the sleep monster.

But Mum couldn't comfort her right now.

Mum *was* the monster.

She was standing on the edge of the metal table that she'd been tied down to just a moment ago.

She wasn't Mum. Not anymore. Her skin was splitting away. Tearing away.

And there was something underneath.

This slimy, gooey, shiny black body, underneath a load of goo, which was dripping off her.

Her eyes were the weirdest things. They kept on moving. They were perfectly black. And when Ava looked into them, for a second, she swore they changed colour. She swore her whole *face* changed. Into hers. Not Mum's. Her *own*.

She started to wonder if this was ever Mum at all. She'd seen her on the table. But maybe it was just her mind playing tricks.

Whatever it was, it wasn't Mum anymore.

It stood over her.

And then it stretched a hand towards her.

This long, black hand.

Only there were no fingers on it.

It was just this long piece of stringy, monstrous rope.

Getting closer to her face.

She was scared. Really scared. Her heart was beating really fast. Her head was spinning. Because—because this was Mum. This was Mum, right here.

And now, Mum had become something else.

Something even scarier.

She climbed over the side of the table.

Looking right down at Ava.

With those big, black eyes.

And those eyes looked… empty. They didn't look real. They were like teddy bear eyes. Like there was no life behind them. Like they were just there for decoration.

She moved her arm closer towards Ava, and Ava felt even more scared.

Even more afraid.

She wanted to get away.

She wanted to run.

But she was…

She was stuck.

Just like she got stuck in the dreams.

She couldn't move.

She could only sit there.

Frozen.

Scared.

Unable to move a muscle.

She felt that arm getting closer.

So close that it was almost touching her face, now.

She watched it inch towards her when…

Suddenly, she remembered.

The angry people.

How they got closer when she was scared.

Just like the monster.

The sleep monster.

The more she tried to get away, the closer it got to her.

The more afraid she got, the closer it got.

She sat there, as this *thing's* arm got closer, and she tried to make her fear go away.

She tried to make it disappear.

But how could she make it disappear?

How?

She sat there and she remembered something Abigail told her, all that time ago.

Something she said her dad had told her.

"Don't push fear away. Let it pass through you."

She felt that fear.

She felt it there.

And even though everything in her body screamed at her to be afraid...

She didn't push against it.

She just felt her racing heart.

She just felt the lump in her throat.

She just felt herself, sweating even more.

Her heart racing even faster.

She felt all these things, as she crouched there, the thing's hand right up to her face.

Almost within touching distance.

She felt the fear.

Right there.

Let it go.

Let... it... go...

Mum's words.

Mum's words, in her head.

She gulped down a big lump in her throat.

She let the fear go.

And then, as that hand got closer to her... she closed her eyes.

And she waited.

She had no idea just yet.

But everything was about to change.

In ways she could not even begin to imagine.

CHAPTER EIGHT

Georgia hadn't seen anyone levitate before.
But she *had* seen a man plummet to his death off a fifteen-storey building before.

And weirdly, this scene in front of her reminded her of that fall, more than anything else.

She'd witnessed it on a night out, walking through town, rather tipsily, towards the cab rank. She was short on change, so she was going to have to borrow some from someone near the stand. Or hope the driver was feeling generous.

And that's when she saw him.

That man.

Standing on top of that building.

Right on the edge of it.

He was shouting stuff. And people were shouting back up at him. It was hard to tell what was being said. Partly because she was tipsy. But partly just because of the intensity of the moment, too.

What she was witnessing.

What she felt she was *about* to witness.

A man.

Falling to his death.

She told herself that wasn't going to happen. That someone was going to talk him down. That everything was going to be okay. Everything was going to work out.

Because things always worked out.

Didn't they?

And then, without any warning—without any dramatic build-up—and in mid-sentence, actually, he simply stepped over the edge of the building, like he was walking over a bridge, and went plummeting to the ground.

She would never forget a lot of things about what she witnessed. The crunching sound of the bones in that poor sod's legs as he hit the ground. The animalistic yelps, as he lay on the ground, barely alive still, spluttering.

But weirdly enough, the thing that stuck with Georgia most was the sight of his legs, kicking desperately, as he stepped over the edge and realised what a horrible mistake he had made.

She was witnessing the same thing right now.

Only it wasn't any man on any rooftop, falling towards the ground.

It was one of Galloway's guards.

First, hovering upwards.

Slowly.

Rising towards the sky.

Staring up at something.

Right up, towards something.

Smiling.

Tears streaming down his face.

But at the same time, as he stared up at whatever was above him... his teeth, chattering.

Ecstasy.

And fear.

Both at once.

She knew there was *something* up there. But she didn't want to look. She wanted to focus on what she could control. Finding Grace's children. Saving them. Stopping *them* from experiencing whatever was going on here, too.

But for the moment, all she could focus on was this man.

Rising.

Rising slowly.

As if a magnet was pulling him closer, and gravity was pulling him back down—as hard as it could.

He paused.

Froze there.

For just a moment.

And then he went surging up towards the sky.

Falling towards the sky.

That was what Georgia noticed above anything.

The way he *fell*.

He wasn't rising.

He was *falling*.

Falling upwards.

Falling into the sky.

Falling off the face of the Earth, into...

No.

She couldn't look up.

She couldn't let herself look up.

Because if she looked up...

She saw Brian again, then.

He was staring up.

But he wasn't rising.

He wasn't floating.

He was just standing there, with Abigail—his daughter—holding on to him.

The dogs around him.

Barking.

Yelping.

And that woman.

The woman by the entrance.

The pregnant woman.

Standing there.

Hand on her pregnant belly.

As if this was normal.

As if all of this was entirely normal.

As if...

That's when Georgia saw it.

Suddenly.

Something started trickling down that woman's legs.

At first, she thought it was blood.

Gathering at her feet.

But when she looked closer, as those sirens rang out, and those screams continued to echo, she realised it wasn't blood.

It was something else.

Something *black*.

This stuff kept pouring out of the woman.

Her pregnant belly began to shrink.

But she didn't seem bothered.

She didn't appear fazed.

If anything...

Her eyes.

Her eyes looked *focused*.

Rolled back into her skull.

Rolled back into her skull, as more of that black stuff oozed out of her, and she craned her neck back, looked up at the sky, and...

No.

No, don't look up.

Even though she felt like there was something up there.

Looking down at her.

Goading her to turn around and check.

She couldn't look up.

She couldn't let herself look up.

She looked at that pregnant woman.

Watched as more of that black stuff pooled out of her.

As her belly got smaller and smaller.

She started shaking, then.

Shaking wildly.

Like she was possessed.

Tensing up.

Veins on the side of her head pulsating.

Spluttering.

Spluttering more of that black stuff.

And gasping.

Gasping and snarling and...

Georgia could only stand there and watch, as this woman's eyes opened again.

Perfectly black.

She could only watch, as she lowered her head to eye level again.

She could only watch, as she looked her in the eye.

Right in the eye.

A smile widened across her face.

Right across her face.

And suddenly, Georgia's urge—her need—to run away kicked in with full force.

But before she could move a muscle, the woman was suddenly in front of her.

She had her cold, slimy hands on the sides of Georgia's head.

And then she leaned in, and pressed her black tongue towards her lips, and...

Everything went bright.

CHAPTER NINE

Brian was in bed again.
He was comfortable. So comfortable. So he should be. He'd spent a lot of money on that bed. The biggest bed possible. The most expensive mattress possible. Kelly told him he must be crazy spending so much on a bed. A bed was a bed, at the end of the day. She wasn't fussy about shit like that. She went travelling a lot, especially in her younger years, and she could doze off on a frigging tree branch if she had to.

And to be honest, Brian used to be the same. He never bought into scams like that. Because, at the end of the day, how much different could sleeping on an expensive, memory foam bed actually be?

And these fancy fucking expensive pillows. Seriously? Just how good could they be?

But he had a bad back. And he was snoring a lot. The doctors told him they suspected he had sleep apnea, and that it might be related to his sleep posture. Or worsened by it, anyway. *Sleep posture.* What a load of shite.

He didn't spend a lot of money. Kelly told him he should treat himself. And if treating himself meant spending shitloads on a fancy bed, then go for it. She wasn't gonna judge. Well. Maybe she *was* gonna judge, a bit.

So he had. He'd pulled the trigger and he'd bought it. He'd got into bed after a night shift, fully expecting to be tossing and turning—he never loved changing beds; he even found sleeping in hotels difficult—and fully expecting his neck to feel just as bad when he woke up, making him regret his damned purchase.

But that didn't happen.

Instead, he woke up fresh as a goddamned daisy.

A whole hour later than he usually did.

So as much as he *wanted* to find something to criticise and something to regret about his insanely overpriced purchase... he couldn't. He just couldn't.

It was a worthy investment.

A really worthy investment.

And that's where he was.

That's exactly where he was right now.

That comfy, spongy memory foam, just soaking him up.

Wrapping around him. Like warm, comforting arms.

He wanted to keep his eyes closed. Because he was warm here. He was comfortable here. He was safe here.

And if he just kept his eyes closed, he could convince himself he was back at home.

Back at home, in bed, with Kelly right beside him.

But the more time passed, the more he felt that delusion slipping away.

He wasn't lying in his bed at all. He wasn't lying on *any* bed. He was on the ground. The cold, hard ground.

His ears were ringing. And he could taste something lingering at the back of his throat. It was coppery. Blood-like.

But there was something different about it, too.

Something slightly *off* about it.

It was hard to explain. But it was as if it wasn't *his* blood. It was someone else's blood. He wasn't sure how he knew that. Why he had that gut feeling. But he did.

He didn't want to open his eyes. He wasn't comfy as it was. But he figured that if he opened his eyes, he was going to feel a whole lot worse. When he saw his surroundings. When he saw the predicament he was in.

When he reminded himself.

But there was a big element of the unknown about all this. And that was because, the last thing he remembered, he was... Wait, where *was* he? He remembered being beaten up. He remembered being dragged into Galloway's safe haven. He remembered... he remembered *Abigail*.

Abigail. And Georgia. And something going down. Something happening.

And...

Emma.

A knot tightened in his stomach when he thought of Emma.

The way she looked.

How pale she was.

How weak she looked.

And that bump on her belly.

That pregnancy bump.

He remembered her, standing there, and an uncertainty washed over him.

But not as hard as the uncertainty about what happened next.

About...

Something happening.

Something happening to Galloway.

Rising up.

Towards the sky.

Towards...

That's where his memory went blank. That's where it all just stopped.

And yet, he *knew* something was there.

Buried down, deep.

He'd witnessed *something*.

He just wasn't sure what it was.

There was something there.

Something buried in his memory.

But he couldn't place it.

He couldn't revisit it.

It was like a mental block.

Like walls had been erected around that memory.

He lay there. On the ground. Ears ringing. A strange smell in the air. A combination of smoke and dew. Morning dew. The smell of rain on a warm day. A freshness. An innocence. Like the world had been reborn again.

Brian lay there, and he pictured all the things he might see when he opened his eyes.

He pictured death.

He pictured chaos.

He pictured destruction.

He gulped.

Shaking.

And then he did the only thing he could do.

He opened his eyes.

He had no idea what he was about to see.

But when he finally *did* see, nothing could have prepared him for the truth.

CHAPTER TEN

Ava stood there, eyes closed, and waited for something to change.

She felt like she was on the top of a rollercoaster. Right before a big drop.

Holding her breath.

Waiting for her tummy to start turning inside out.

But...

The longer she stood there, eyes closed, heart beating fast... she felt like she was stuck at the top of the rollercoaster.

Stuck, waiting for that weird *thing* that had come out of Mum to touch her.

To grab her face.

To do something to her.

Something horrible to her.

The seconds felt like forever. But she kept on waiting.

And waiting.

And waiting.

And the more she waited, the more she wondered.

What if?

What if nothing happened?

What if the *thing* was just waiting for her to open her eyes?

To look right at it?

She had no idea how long she stood there.

Heart thumping.

Eyes squeezed shut.

Perched at the top of that rollercoaster.

Ready to plummet over the edge.

But she knew she was going to have to open her eyes.

She knew it was time.

She couldn't stand here forever.

She felt that fear in her tummy.

She looked at it.

She watched it.

She didn't let it take over her.

She *couldn't* let it take over her.

She just had to watch it.

Let it sit there.

Look after it.

Like it was a pet.

She gulped down a lump in her throat.

And then she opened her eyes.

She expected to see that creature.

The horrible thing that had dragged itself out of Mum's body.

She expected to see her right in front of her.

Peering into her eyes with those weird, jet-black eyes of her own.

She expected to see that long, weird arm stretching closer towards her.

And teeth.

Big, sharp teeth.

But Ava didn't see any of those things.

Any of those things at all.

The red lights were still flashing. On and off.

She could still hear this weird noise. Not the same noise she'd heard before. Something different. Something new.

But every time that light flickered on, every time the room lit up—all red—she didn't see Mum.

She didn't see Mum at all.

Or that monster.

She didn't see anyone in here.

She saw blood.

And she saw bits of skin.

Bits of meat on the ground.

But other than that...

Nothing.

There was nothing else in here.

No one else in here.

Only her.

She didn't want to get too far ahead of herself. Because maybe she was wrong. Maybe that monster was hiding. Maybe it was behind her. Waiting to jump out at her. Waiting to scare her.

But the longer she stood there, heart racing, letting the fear sit there, but not letting it take over her, she started to realise that she was definitely alone.

There was no one else in this room.

No one else here.

She looked around. Slowly. Watched as the red lights lit the place up. The alarms were still ringing. Really loud. Making her head spin.

She looked right around the room. Right around this darkness. And she still couldn't see anyone. There was no one hiding in here. No one at all.

But she didn't understand. It didn't make sense. How could there be no one here?

Because that monster. It was right opposite her just a few minutes ago. Right in front of her.

So where was it now?

She stood there. Her tummy feeling weird. She looked over at that door. The door out of this room. She wasn't sure she wanted to go through there. Because that's where the monster must've gone. There was nowhere else it could've gone.

She tasted something weird in her mouth. Something she had never tasted before. It was a bit like metal. Mixed with something else. Something she couldn't place. She couldn't even tell if it was nice or not. If she liked it or not.

But it made her feel a bit weird.

She looked at that door, as she stood in the middle of the darkness. And even though she was scared about leaving this room, and finding whatever was out there, she knew she couldn't stay here any longer.

She knew what she had to do.

She walked.

Towards that door.

Slowly.

The red lights flashing, on and off.

On, and off, and on, and off.

And that siren, ringing out.

She got to the door. She looked back into the darkness of the room. On the floor, by the table, she saw blood. Skin. Meat.

She didn't want to think about what it was. Who it was from.

Mum.

She didn't want to think of it as being all that was left of her.

She wiped away her tears.

Mum had been gone a long time.

That was how she had to think now.

She turned around, and she stepped towards the door.

She peeked into the corridor.

It was dark in here, too.

The red lights were flashing, the same as in the smaller room.

And this corridor was really long. It stretched right on, into the distance.

And anything could be hiding in the shadows.

Waiting for her.

She looked down the corridor, towards the door.

The way out of here.

She felt the fear growing.

She felt it building inside her.

She gulped.

She took a deep breath.

And then she walked.

Her legs were like jelly.

Every step she took, she swore she saw movement in the corners of her eyes.

Or heard things, scuttling along the walls.

Chasing her.

She walked faster. But when she did that, she saw and heard these things even more. And she felt even more scared.

And she didn't want that.

It was like the sleep demon.

She couldn't try and escape it.

She just had to keep going.

Keep on going.

She kept on walking and walking until she reached the steps.

And then the door.

The way out of here.

She climbed up them.

She didn't want to look back.

But she looked back anyway.

She turned around.

Saw the darkness.

And saw that red light.

Flashing on, and off.

On, and off.

And when it flashed off, just this once, she swore she saw something.

Staring at her in the dark shadows.

She turned around.

She gulped.

She walked up to the door.

She didn't know what she was going to find behind the door.

She didn't know what to expect.

She pushed the door open.

As hard as she could.

It took her eyes a few seconds to understand what she was looking at, outside that door.

But when she realised what it was... Ava didn't know what to think.

About anything.

CHAPTER ELEVEN

Everything went bright.

And then, in a flash—a literal flash—Georgia could *see* again.

There are some times in life when you truly cannot comprehend what you are witnessing. When, upon seeing something, your reality halts for a moment. A pure moment in time where nothing makes sense. And all you can do is witness. Witness, without processing. Like a computer trying to figure its way through a glitch.

For Georgia, this was one of those moments.

It was light, for one. Which was... unusual. Unusual, to say the least. The sun. Shining down from above. Bright blue skies. Not a cloud in sight.

She could see birds. Flying above. She could hear them singing, too. Sure, the alarms were still ringing out. Those sirens.

But no more screams.

No more gunshots.

Just...

Serenity.

Peace.

She blinked a few times and wondered if she was dead. Was this heaven? She wasn't sure she believed in heaven. She liked the idea of it. The thought of life after death. A place where everything was okay. Where everything was good.

But it seemed far-fetched, didn't it? Not to shit on religion. But if humanity itself was there... then what chance was there of that place being good at all?

People would find ways to fall out, and conquer, and dominate, and form themselves into hierarchical structures, over and over and over again.

It'd always been that way.

And it always would be that way.

And no heaven could change that fact.

She was lying on the ground. The ground felt quite warm underneath her face. She could taste the dirt in her mouth. She'd been lying right against it. Practically kissing it. Her ears were ringing. Her head, banging. She felt weak. So fucking weak. She was dehydrated. Starving. And still in pain, after being strung up by Galloway—a moment that felt like forever ago.

She thought of Galloway.

And then of Grace.

Of the promise she'd made her, as her life faded, in her arms.

The promise to find her children.

To protect them.

But then she was back to thinking of Galloway again.

She'd seen something. She'd seen him... levitating. There was no other way of putting it. She'd seen him levitating. And other people levitating, too.

No. Not levitating.

Falling.

Falling upwards, towards the sky.

And then...

She'd seen this woman.

This pregnant woman.

Ghostlike.

Black slop seeping out of her.

Giving birth to...

Something.

She blinked again, a few more times, trying to understand how any time had passed since then—because it didn't feel like a single moment had passed—and she looked around.

She was lying right where she'd been standing in her last memory. Right by the entrance to this safe zone.

Grace's body was lying there. Right beside her.

Her pretty eyes staring at her, widely.

Empty.

Dead.

She turned around, expecting to see more bodies. Expecting to see... well, she didn't know *what* she was expecting to see.

But she wasn't expecting to see what she *did* see.

There were a few people around her. Lying down. Just like her.

She blinked a few times. Her vision drifting back.

And when she blinked, she realised these weren't just anyone.

They were the people she knew.

Brian.

Abigail.

The dogs were up and about. Wagging their tails. Tongues dangling out. One of them—a little pug-type one—barked at her, and wagged its bum excitedly.

She stroked it with her weak, shaking hand. Then she looked over at the people. Lying there.

She saw Brian lifting his head, and relief hit her.

Hard.

She wanted to go over to him. To hug him. Pretty damned hard. He was alive. Still alive. After all this time.

She stumbled up to her feet. Somehow, she felt even weaker than before. Like she'd just woken up from a deep sleep. Groggy. Lethargic. Not quite with it. And even though she was relieved to see Brian again—and he and his daughter reunited, no less—she still felt distracted.

Distracted, by the absurdity of everything.

She looked back. Around at the entrance area of the safe zone.

It was quiet.

Surprisingly so.

There was no one around.

Not that she could see.

One or two guards in the distance. Who looked like *they* were waking up from something, too.

There was no sign of Galloway.

She turned back around and headed towards Brian and Abigail, and she noticed someone else was missing.

The woman.

The pregnant woman.

There was no sign of her.

No sign that she had ever been here at all.

It unsettled her. Made her question whether what she had seen was real at all. Or whether *this* now was even real at all.

She just didn't know what to believe.

But that momentary sense of confusion—and that overwhelming urge to help Grace's children—was suddenly replaced by the very fact that Brian was standing right in front of her.

He looked at her with wide eyes. He looked thinner. Badly beaten. But it was him. No doubt about it.

She hugged him. Tight. And then backed off a little, when she realised she was hurting him. And hurting herself, too.

And then Abigail hugged them both. Which was... bizarre. She barely knew Abigail. But they were bound by shared trauma. The shared trauma of being locked away together in this place.

When they finished hugging, reality hit hard again.

The quietness.

The strange, sudden transition from night to day.

"Do you remember... anything?" Georgia asked.

Brian and Abigail both looked at her. Wide-eyed. Confused. Confirming that it wasn't just her going through the same sense of confusion.

"Just the siren," Abigail said. "Then Galloway. The sky. And…"

She shook her head.

Her memory, failing, right where Georgia's had failed.

And seemingly where Brian's had failed, too.

She looked around at the silent, empty base.

No more gunfire.

A siren ringing, sure.

But that was very much just a part of the background, now.

They all stood there.

Silent.

Speechless.

The absurdity of the situation dampening the reunion, somewhat.

She looked up at the sky.

A blue sky.

A normal, beautiful blue sky.

She waited for someone to fill the silence.

For just one of them to speak.

It was Brian.

And his words perfectly captured everything she was feeling right now.

"What the fuck did we just witness?" he said.

A soft breeze picked up.

Georgia shivered.

It was warm.

It was perfect.

Everything was so perfect.

But one thing was for certain.

One thing was a given.

Something was wrong.

Very wrong.

CHAPTER TWELVE

Brian had visited a real-life ghost town once before.

It was on a trip to the Balkans with Kelly. Truth be told, he wasn't majorly fussed about going over that way. He was a bit boring when it came to holidays. He didn't like anywhere too dangerous. Anywhere too risky. And by that, he meant he only really liked package holidays. Beach holidays. Boring, touristy holidays.

So when Kelly suggested a trip to the Balkans, it was safe to say they didn't quite fall in with Brian's idea of safe and boring.

He'd had a good time, though, to be fair. His fears proved pretty much unwarranted. The people were lovely. The scenery was incredible. The food and drinks were extra cheap, too. Had some of the best meals of his life there.

The highlight, though, was a trip to a ghost town. A town that people just got up and abandoned because the economic opportunity just slipped away from the area in a flash during the wars.

It was eerie. He thought he was prepared for it. Thought he knew exactly what to expect. He'd seen quiet towns before, plenty of times.

But there's something truly unsettling about a town that had literally gone quiet overnight.

The reminders of life.

Cars in the drive, now covered in dust.

Half-eaten meals, still sitting there on the table, devoured by the flies and the rats.

Beds unmade.

Calendars unchanged.

He'd seen plenty of sights like this since the outbreak unfolded. Plenty of ghost towns.

But nothing quite as eerie as the one he was walking through right now.

The sun was beaming down really strong, really bright. His heart wouldn't stop racing. Everywhere he looked, he expected to see someone. For someone to come launching out. Infected, or otherwise.

But nobody did.

This place looked like it used to be a pretty active safe zone. A community. There were signs that there had been life here. Signs that this place had been lived in, fairly recently.

But all of that had changed.

He held on to Abigail's hand, as he walked through this old town. It still seemed surreal. The very fact that he was holding his daughter's hand at all. It felt like they had so much talking to do. So much catching up to do. Making up for lost time. Healing rifts. Building bridges.

But, in another sense, that didn't really feel necessary at all.

In some ways, all that mattered was that she was here.

She was right here.

The time for catching up—for healing any rifts—would come.

Those rifts paled in comparison to what they were going through now.

What they were witnessing now.

They walked slowly through this abandoned town. Although

"abandoned' was technically the wrong way of looking at it, wasn't it? Something had happened here. He didn't know what. One moment, he had been staring up into the sky, at... *something*. Something he couldn't remember.

And then the next moment...

Waking up on the concrete.

In the daylight.

And the place suddenly seemed a lot quieter.

A whole lot quieter.

Especially since the sirens had stopped ringing now, too.

Georgia walked along with him and Abigail. The dogs followed, too. He wanted to keep them close. All of them close. It might be quiet here. But something wasn't right. Something just didn't *feel* right. It felt off.

It might be sunny. It might be quiet. And on the surface, it might not *seem* like there was anything to worry about.

But that's what was weird about it.

He'd grown so accustomed to being on edge all the time that the sense that things were *normal* unsettled him deeply.

Especially when he didn't have a clue how it had got to this point.

The more they walked through these streets—silent, observant—the more it dawned on Brian that something truly unexpected had happened. He saw people. They all saw people. Crouched there on the ground. Disorientated. Guards, by the looks of things. Rubbing their eyes. Holding their helmets.

And other people. Lying there. Unconscious.

But it soon became clear to Brian, as he made his way through these streets, that his gut feeling was correct.

"There should be more than this," Abigail said.

Brian looked at her. He didn't know exactly what she meant by that. But he could figure it out.

"More what?" Georgia asked.

Abigail gulped. Quite visibly. Stared on, with wide eyes. "More people," she said.

It spoke to him when she said those words. It really did feel like something had been *taken* from this place. Some of it had been left over. Themselves included.

But something had been *taken*, too.

He thought of Emma, and his skin turned cold.

He'd seen her. Absolutely no fucking doubt about it.

Walking in through those gates.

Standing there.

Holding her pregnant belly.

He wondered if he'd hallucinated her. If she'd ever been there at all. Only when Abigail and Georgia confirmed they'd seen her too did he know she was real.

And that in itself seemed... impossible. He hadn't seen her in ages. Since the very beginning. That night. That night when she'd confided in him. Confided in him about her abusive relationship.

And then she'd just gone.

She'd just disappeared.

In the night.

So her arrival. Her very arrival.

That in itself was uncanny.

Made even weirder by the fact she had disappeared.

He walked up to the balcony area where Galloway had stood, what felt like just moments ago.

There was no sign of him.

He wasn't here.

Not anymore.

The last Brian could remember?

Galloway, looking up into the sky.

Looking up in wide-eyed amazement.

Then, looking back down.

Right at Brian.

His eyes bloodshot.

Crying.

"Don't look up."

And...

And then, after that, everything was blurry.

He stood there and looked at where Galloway had stood. If he'd disappeared, he had mixed emotions about that. He still had a score to settle with him. For what he'd done. For what his people had done.

But... even *that* felt like it paled in comparison, now.

He looked up at where Galloway disappeared.

Then, up at the sky.

That perfect blue sky.

He saw birds flying across it.

The light of the sun, beaming across it.

He took a long, deep breath, and he swallowed a lump in his throat.

"Come on," he said. "Let's keep..."

Then, from the left, he heard something.

A voice.

A childlike voice.

"Brian?" it said.

He turned around.

Suddenly.

He looked at where that voice was coming from.

And when he saw who was standing there, right before him... he could barely suppress the smile from breaking across his face.

And the tears from building in his eyes.

It was *her*.

CHAPTER THIRTEEN

When Ava stepped out of the horrible tunnel where all the awful things had happened, the first thing that struck her was just how sunny it was. Just how bright it was. And it amazed her that it was daytime all of a sudden. She didn't think she'd been in that room where Mum was for too long. She had no idea how so much time had passed so quickly. Usually, that only ever happened when she was enjoying something. Like when she was at a theme park, or a water park, or on the PlayStation with Dad.

She definitely hadn't been enjoying herself when she was stuck in that dark room with Mum.

If anything, time should have gone really, really, really slowly in there.

But it was daytime. A really nice day, too. A sunny day. Birds were flying around in the sky. The annoying siren noise had stopped, too. She couldn't hear it anymore.

She couldn't hear much. Any guns. Or any screams. Or anything like that.

Everything was just...

Really quiet.

And Ava knew that should be a good thing. Because that was all she wanted, wasn't it? Somewhere nice. Somewhere safe.

Maybe something had happened to make the angry people stop being angry. Maybe some powerful people had used a special weapon and killed all the angry people. Maybe they were gone now.

But as she stood there, she didn't know. It didn't matter how much she thought about it. She just didn't have a clue.

She just thought of Mum.

She felt sad when she thought of Mum. She'd spent so long hoping she was still out there. Hoping that she would find her again, someday.

And she had. She had been here. All along.

But...

She thought of that woman, lying on that table.

In pain.

Struggling.

Suffering.

That woman wasn't Mum.

Not anymore.

The Mum she knew—the Mum she remembered and loved—she was gone.

She wished she had been able to help her. To stop what happened to her.

That *thing*.

Bursting out of her body.

She wished she had been able to stop that, before it happened.

But she hadn't.

She hadn't been able to do that.

Mum was gone.

She stood there. At the entrance to this place where she'd run. Things *felt* different from when she'd run inside, after she'd escaped the restaurant place. Did she have something to do with that? Pressing that button? She didn't know. She didn't know *what* she'd done, or *what* had happened. She couldn't really remember properly. Just that Mum had got in her head, and...

It all went blurry after that. Really blurry.

Like a dream.

A dream that she couldn't remember properly.

She stood at the entrance to this place and noticed something on the ground. Patches. Weird patches. They looked a bit like that goo. Like sticky goo.

Or blood.

It was hard to tell.

And there were a few of these patches.

Little patches, on the ground, underneath her.

Patches that definitely weren't there before.

She looked down at them, and she didn't know what they were. They were weird. Really weird. And they just made her feel even more strange. The daylight. These patches. And how *quiet* everything seemed.

And the way that monster had disappeared, too.

The one that had crawled out of Mum.

What was happening?

She got a taste in her mouth, then. That weird taste again. Only this time... this time, it reminded her of a nosebleed. When her nose was bleeding, and leaking back into her throat, she could taste it. Strong, and horrible.

But this was a little bit different. That other taste was there, too. The one she couldn't explain. The one she couldn't describe.

The one that just reminded her of that arm, reaching towards her, and...

She heard movement down the street.

She turned around. Heart beating faster. Even though she needed to stay calm.

She expected angry people.

She expected monsters.

Or even just Galloway's people.

She expected all kinds of things. Horrible things.

But when she saw exactly who it was... she couldn't stop herself from blinking, hard, to make sure she definitely wasn't imagining them.

The more she blinked, the clearer they became.

They weren't disappearing.

They weren't disappearing at all.

They were real.

They were very real.

And they were right here.

A woman she didn't recognise, first.

Skinny.

Slim.

Pale.

And then...

Two people she *did* recognise.

And four *dogs* she recognised, too.

She looked at them all, heart racing, and then she looked at the man leading the group, and she could hardly hold back her tears.

"Brian?" she said.

She thought he wasn't going to hear her. She thought something was going to be wrong. She thought he might be an angry person in disguise. Or that something might break out of him. Just like it had broken out of Mum.

But he looked at her.

He looked right at her.

Time paused.

Stood still.

The longer it stood still... the more worried Ava got.

What if this was wrong?

What if this was all wrong?

But then, he blinked.

He blinked, and he looked right at her.

Right into her eyes.

"Ava?" he said. His voice shaking.

She looked at him.

She smiled at him.

Smiled right back at him.

Tears clouding her eyes.

This wasn't in her head.

And it wasn't wrong.

This was *real*.

It was actually real.

Brian was here.

Abigail was here.

And the dogs were here, too.

She wasn't sure how long she stood there.

Frozen.

Feeling a warmth growing within.

Feeling her excitement build.

Like she was right at the top of that rollercoaster again, getting ready to drop.

"Brian," she said. Again.

And then, she didn't remember what happened next.

Because she just ran towards them—towards the people, and towards the dogs, as they came running at her, ears back, as a smile stretched across her face, and tears streamed down her cheeks.

For the first time in forever... Ava felt like she was *home*.

Far away in the distance, clouds began to gather.

CHAPTER FOURTEEN

There were very few things that Georgia had ever witnessed that she could truly describe as "beautiful."

Emma and Joe's wedding. *That* was beautiful. Childhood sweethearts. Met when they were four. Together officially when they were eleven. Married in their early twenties. It was gorgeous to witness something so enduring. True, pure love. Something that would never go sour.

Only it did, when Joe's porn addiction came out, and it turned out Emma had been fucking a bloke from work.

But even so. The sentiment was what mattered, right?

It was beautiful.

Truly beautiful.

There had been a few other moments like that. Seeing the neighbours' puppy, Lucy, walk again, after extensive spinal surgery. Wagging her little tail. *That* was beautiful. And it came with no stinger, either.

Just beauty.

Pure, unfiltered beauty.

But this right here.

This moment right here.

This was beauty.

That little girl. She looked pale. Bruised. She looked weak. Georgia wasn't certain, but she could only assume that she'd been captive here, somewhere.

She looked ahead, with wide eyes.

And for some reason, before Brian even said a word, she knew who this kid was.

Ava.

The girl. The girl Brian had been looking for. The one he'd sworn he would locate. That he'd sworn and vowed he would find.

She was right here.

And she was running towards Brian.

The dogs were running towards her.

All of them, wagging their tails.

And Brian was staggering towards her, too.

And as Georgia stood there, under this blue sky, with Abigail beside her... she almost had to pinch herself.

These reunions.

All these reunions.

They seemed... almost *too* good to be true.

But she couldn't deny what she was witnessing.

What was happening.

It might seem too good to be true.

But it *was* true.

She watched them run towards each other, and tears welled up in her eyes. Rather selfishly, as much as she adored this reunion—because it really was beautiful—it struck her then that she could never have a reunion like this someday. Her parents were gone. Her friends were long gone. And no partners. She had no one from her past. Which was probably why she had been so elated when she had seen Brian again. And seeing what she was witnessing right now.

She stood there, watching the dogs jump up with joy, as Brian hugged Ava, and she felt something.

A hand.

Against hers.

She looked down.

She saw Abigail.

Not looking at her.

But holding her hand.

Holding her hand, looking at this scene too, also welling up.

Almost as if she was inviting her into this moment.

Allowing her to feel a sense of connection from it, too.

She didn't know a lot about Abigail. She'd barely had a conversation with her. Only that she was Brian's daughter. She was tough. Incredibly tough. And she had her guilt. Her guilt, about leaving someone behind. About failing someone.

She hoped that she'd be able to move past some of her guilt now her and her dad had been reunited.

Once they figured out what the hell was going on here, anyway.

She thought about the kids, then. Grace's kids. Fuck. The realisation hit her square in the chest. She needed to go find them. She needed to check on them. She needed to get to them. She'd promised Grace that much. That's what she had to do. Exactly what she had to do.

She watched this scene unfold. And as much as she wanted to be involved... she squeezed Abigail's hand a little tighter, then let go.

Abigail glanced around at her.

"There's something I need to do," Georgia said. "Somewhere... somewhere I need to be."

Abigail looked like she was going to ask her where. Like she was going to query her.

But instead, she just stayed silent, stared right at her, and nodded.

Georgia looked back at Brian again. Ava again. The dogs again.

She saw their happiness.

She saw their joy.

And she prayed it lasted.

She turned around, and she began her walk towards the place Grace had told her Theo and Elizabeth, her children, were being held.

It was only when she was a few steps away that Abigail finally spoke.

"Be careful," she said.

Georgia looked around at her.

Abigail wasn't looking at her anymore.

Instead, she was staring right ahead.

"Just... just be careful," she said.

She didn't say what she had to be careful about.

She didn't have to.

Georgia wasn't stupid.

She *knew* something had happened.

She knew something was different.

Very, very different.

She swallowed a lump in her throat.

She nodded.

And then she turned around and walked towards the place where Theo and Elizabeth were being held.

For Grace.

She wasn't sure if she was imagining things.

If her mind was playing tricks on her.

But she could have sworn she saw movement, in the shadows, in the corners of her eyes...

CHAPTER FIFTEEN

Brian wanted this moment of reunion to last forever.

He wanted to hold Ava. And Abigail. He wanted to stroke the dogs. And then there was Georgia, too. He wanted to stay in this moment. He wanted to luxuriate in it. Forever.

But he couldn't.

Because, as much as he tried to convince himself that everything was okay now... the very fact of his existence was a reminder that something was wrong.

Very wrong.

He looked around the street. It looked empty. As mentioned, it was like a ghost town. It hadn't exactly been bustling with life before. It was the middle of the night when he'd got here, after all.

But it had certainly felt like there was a *potential* for life here.

It felt like a sleeping town, rather than a dead town.

He could see crows, swooping overhead. A sign that death was looming. He could hear them cawing every now and then. And their caws cut through the silence. An eerie silence. He could hear the dogs panting. Ghost, whining a little. Like he was unsure. Deeply unsettled about something.

There was a strange smell in the air. It smelled like a stuffy room, with all the windows shut, on a summer's day. Heating on. A kind of *sweaty* smell, almost. Like the air was carrying something. Something thick. Something heavy.

Something that felt like it was on the brink of bursting out.

A bitter taste crossed his lips. He felt weak. Shaky. It was hardly a surprise. He'd been battered not long ago. Stabbed, too. He'd been through it. Right through it. And then there was the emotional rollercoaster he'd been on ever since. The reunions. So many reunions.

And then the small matter of the *incident*, bang in the middle.

He thought back to that moment.

To the moment everything changed.

To Galloway.

Looking up at the sky.

Then, looking back down at him.

Right into his eyes.

Tears streaming down his weathered cheeks.

Catching on his perfectly trimmed beard.

Dangling on his lower eyelashes.

Two expressions on his face.

One of elation.

One of fear.

And then...

Falling.

And after that, a faint fuzziness, and then darkness.

It left an even more bitter taste in Brian's mouth. Merely the thought of it.

There were too many unanswered questions.

And Brian couldn't deal with unanswered questions like this.

He held on to Ava. She was thin. Very thin. She was crying a lot, too. It seemed like she had been suppressing these tears. The poor kid. Brian didn't know what she'd been through. What she'd witnessed. But it was safe to assume it hadn't been a fucking walk in the park for her. It couldn't have been a walk in the park for *anyone* who was still here.

He looked at her. Right into her tearful, bloodshot eyes.

And she stared back at him.

Stared back at him with a combination of relief, and again, of fear.

She wasn't saying anything. She just seemed... confused. And Brian could understand it. He felt that confusion, too. The shift. From night to day. That great *emptiness*.

He couldn't explain it.

He couldn't even *begin* to explain it.

But something had happened.

And he wasn't the only one who had experienced it.

He realised then, upon looking back at her, that Ava wasn't looking at him anymore.

She was looking *beyond* him.

She was looking at someone behind him.

Someone standing right behind him.

She was looking at *Abigail*.

Brian looked around at Abigail.

His daughter.

His beautiful daughter, who he still couldn't believe was here at all.

They'd barely even spoken. They hadn't had a chance to. Nobody had, really. They were all in a trance. A collective trance. After what had happened. What they'd witnessed. What they'd seen.

But Abigail.

Ava.

The way they looked at one another.

That was a look of recognition.

And then Brian remembered what Ava told him. About her being out there. About *meeting* her, even.

Suddenly, everything felt like it was clicking into place.

But the way they looked at each other.

The way they stared into one another's eyes.

It didn't look like a happy reunion.

A reunion without depth to it.

Without complexities.

It looked like one with many, many layers.

Layers that he couldn't even begin to understand.

He saw them both standing there. Frozen. In stasis.

Realisation sinking in, with each of them.

And then, out of nowhere, he saw Abigail open her mouth and say something he wasn't entirely used to her saying.

"I'm so sorry," she said.

She stepped forward.

She held Ava.

And Ava hugged her, too.

Hugged her, and cried into her arms.

"I never should have left you," Abigail said.

"It's okay," Ava said.

"No. No, it's not okay. I was supposed to be looking after you. I just… I got scared. I didn't think I could do it. And I couldn't bear to lose you. I'm sorry."

They held each other. And all Brian could do was stand there. All he could do was watch.

Because even though they were all uncertain—even though nobody knew what in the name of fuck was going on here—right now, this was all that mattered.

All that mattered at all.

He looked down at Abigail and Ava, and at the dogs, all of them here, all of them together, all of them happy.

And then he looked right over at where Galloway had risen to the sky.

Tumbled towards the sky.

He swallowed a lump in his throat.

A creeping sensation, crawling up his skin.

And in the bright blue above, he sensed all was not as it seemed.

CHAPTER SIXTEEN

Galloway opened his eyes.
But he might as well not have opened his eyes.
Because all he saw was darkness.
Total, pitch-black darkness.

He tried moving his eyes. Tried looking left and right. Up and down. But it didn't matter how much he moved his eyes. Everything was dark. So, so dark.

He noted then that this wasn't like the sort of pitch-black he was used to. The kind of pitch-black he'd seen before. This wasn't the darkness of night. This was pure sensory deprivation, when it came to sight. It wasn't even like darkness, in a way. It was as if his ability to *see* had been completely switched off.

And something else had been switched off, too.

That was his ability to *remember*.

It sounded far-fetched, but it was true. He couldn't remember how he'd got to where he was—wherever this was. But, strangely enough, as much as the idea of losing all sense of where he was, and even, to a degree, of *who* he was, was terrifying... he felt rather relaxed. Rather calm. Relatively at ease, all things considered.

He could hear something. A low hum. It was a sound he had heard before, somewhere. It felt internal. Like tinnitus. A condition he had long acclimatised to. He had "suffered" with it all his life. Honestly, he didn't know there was any other way of existing. He thought *everyone* lived with a slight hum in their ears at all times.

But this hum. This hum was different.

This hum, he *did* remember.

The O.R.I.O.N Project. Vesperium. It all came flooding back.

The discovery he'd made.

The research programs.

The attempts that were being made, by scientists, deep underground.

Attempts to *make contact*.

Make contact with *something*...

And Galloway had found himself at the forefront of those efforts. He'd found himself testing on people. Testing Vesperium —the substance—on people in different ways. He'd infected people with it. He'd watched them change. He'd found ways to harness it. To resist it. To hold the infected back. Ways to play God.

But there was still one thing missing.

The Threshold Event.

How to activate it.

He had read the theories. The theories about certain people being more *receptive*.

And he'd wanted to *believe* that he was one of those people, too.

Because whatever was out there. They were communicating with him.

They were trying to reach this place.

Through him.

Like a beacon.

But...

He remembered something, now.

Sudden.

A shiver creeping up his spine.

Staring up into the sky.

Seeing something up there.

Something looking down at him.

Something looking right down at him, as his feet lifted off the ground, and...

And then everything went blurry.

After that point, everything went blank.

And now...

This.

He blinked again. A few times. He tried to see something in the darkness. He tried to squint. He tried to see.

But nothing was there.

Nothing but the darkness.

Nothing but...

This humming.

Nothing but...

He noticed something, then.

It was hard to explain. Because he almost felt as if he had lost all sense of his body. Of where his different body parts were.

But...

He had this distinct sense that something was blocking his nostrils.

And that something was in his throat.

Deep in his throat.

Stopping him from breathing.

Panic kicked in, then. His heart started racing. Pounding. Fast. Hard.

He couldn't breathe.

He couldn't breathe, and he was going to suffocate.

He was going to choke.

He was going to...

He felt something else, then.

This *warmth*.

Seeping down his throat.

And it was almost as if whatever it was, it was calming him down.

Reassuring him.

Thick. And comforting.

Like warm milk.

A memory he didn't even know he had. Of being at his mother's breast.

Of drinking that milk.

Feeling it trickle into his mouth.

Down his throat.

Into his belly.

Warming him.

Comforting him.

He felt this warmth filling his body, and somehow, the fear drifted away.

Somehow, he could feel the fear just…

Dissipating.

Vanishing.

Inside him.

Logically, Galloway *wanted* to resist that warmth.

He *wanted* to push it away.

In the same way as he hated anaesthetic, because it stripped him of his illusion of control, he didn't want this.

It felt like it was dulling his senses.

Like it was numbing him.

But as much as he wanted to resist it, logically… he couldn't.

He could only let it flow.

Let it keep filling his veins.

Let it keep *calming* him.

Let it…

That was when he saw something.

It was only brief.
But it was right there.
Right in front of him.
Almost so brief that he couldn't even comprehend it.
But he saw it.
And he *did* comprehend it.
To a degree.
He could see the sky.
The sky was above him.
And it looked like it was moving.
Like the clouds were moving past him.
Fast.
He looked up at that sky and realised he was lying down.
He was lying on his back.
And…
He was naked.
He was naked, and…
He wasn't alone.
There were people.
People all lined up beside him.
People he recognised.
People he didn't.
All lined up.
All naked.
And all with these long, slimy, black *things*, sticking into their mouths, and…
He looked back around, and he realised something.
Something hit him. With disorienting intensity.
The sense that he was lying down.
That he was looking *up* at the sky.
Suddenly, that reversed in a flash.
A sickening flash.
A flash that filled him with a renewed fear, all over again.
Because…

He wasn't looking *up* at the sky.

He was looking *down*.

He was hovering, and he was looking back *down,* towards the sky, from...

Suddenly, it came to mind.

Suddenly, it flashed into his memory.

The memory.

The memory of what he'd seen.

The memory of what he'd seen when he'd looked up at the sky, and...

His heart started racing.

The fear started racing.

The fear, replacing the warmth, and the suffocation, and...

As soon as he felt the fear...

That sensation, again.

That sensation in his throat.

That warmth in his throat.

The memories growing fragmented. Like a rainbow upon approach. Like a dream upon awakening. Like a thought upon inspection.

He tried to cling to them.

He tried to cling to his awareness.

He tried to grip onto it.

He tried to stop it slipping away...

And then he felt that warmth surrounding him, and the darkness blanketing him, and everything was okay again...

Darkness.

Silence.

Bliss.

CHAPTER SEVENTEEN

Ava held on to Abigail and wondered if she was dreaming.

Because even though everything felt good again... there was still a feeling, deep inside her, that something was wrong.

Very wrong.

It was the taste in her mouth that made her realise that something wasn't right. Wasn't normal. It was a kind of bitter taste. It didn't really remind her of anything. But if it reminded her of *one* thing—and only very slightly—it was some biscuits she'd eaten back in winter.

She was on her own. In this house. She was so hungry. But she didn't want to eat some of the rat she'd caught and cooked. The way that Abigail had taught her how to catch. She wanted something lighter on her tummy. Which was weird, because she *was* hungry. She just... wanted something *normal*. Some cake. Or a burger. Or some biscuits.

She would never forget the delight she had felt when she had walked into that old, dusty kitchen and found those biscuits in that cupboard. Opening that lid. Licking her lips. Getting ready to crunch down on them. Imagining all the ways they were going to taste, even though they didn't look that special.

And then biting down on them and realising how soft they were.

And how they had turned a weird blue colour on the top.

Blue and furry.

She felt sick at the memory of it. She felt sick at the time, too.

And yet, she couldn't stop eating those biscuits.

She couldn't stop herself.

She wondered if that was how the angry people felt, when they were ripping into people.

When they were biting through the skin.

Tasting flesh.

She wondered if *they* wanted to eat people. Whether they were really enjoying it.

Or if it was like her and the biscuits.

She didn't know.

She hoped she would never find out.

Abigail was holding her. She was crying. Saying sorry. Ava had never seen her this sad before. This open before. It made her feel a bit weird. Abigail was tough. She was strong. She was never fun. And she never seemed sad like this, either. She could tell she felt bad about leaving Ava, which she had confirmed she had done right away. Something to do with worrying that she wasn't going to be able to look after her. Ava didn't know if that was true or not. She wasn't entirely sure it even mattered.

What mattered was that she was here now.

And that Brian was here, too.

Father and daughter.

And all the dogs.

Only...

The things she'd seen.

Mum.

On that metal table.

The black goo coming out of her body.

And then…

Something making her walk over to that computer, and do things she didn't even understand.

And then…

It was all blurry after that.

But she knew she'd seen something.

Something horrible.

And then it was daytime again.

She felt Abigail's hands on her back. Holding her. Tight. She knew she should feel happy. She should feel good. Because this *was* good. Seeing these people. Seeing all these people again.

But there was something else.

Something inside her.

That taste.

That weird taste.

That taste that wouldn't go away.

She thought about the weird patches she'd seen on the ground.

Then, she thought about the weird things she'd seen, all that time ago.

The weird round ball.

The people.

All dangling from *something*…

And…

She thought about Mum.

"It's going to be okay now," Abigail said. "Everything is going to be okay."

She thought about Abigail's words.

She saw the dogs.

And Brian.

She saw all these things.

And she wanted to believe Abigail.

She really did.

She didn't notice. Not right at that moment.

But Ghost wasn't looking at Ava like he usually did.

Ghost wasn't looking at her like he did when he first saw her again, after all this time.

The hairs on Ghost's back were up.

And even though she didn't hear it—even though none of them heard it...

Ghost was growling at her.

CHAPTER EIGHTEEN

Georgia knew she shouldn't go walking off on her own.
But some habits were hard to kill.
It went back to childhood. She was always *that* kid. The one who went wandering in the supermarket. The whole world was her playground at that age. Around every corner, a potential discovery to be made. New sights. New sounds. New tastes.

But when she realised she had walked away from Mum, *again*, the panic would always set in. The mad panic of realisation. Realising she had walked away from her. Realising she had lost her.

Eventually, though, after a few minutes of pure fear, she would find her again. Mum would always be concerned. Some horrible case on the news, where a child had wandered off with some boys, who had gone on to kill him. That had filtered her worries.

But still, she walked.
Still, she wandered.
Still, she explored.
Until the day everything changed.
She finished school early. It was some sort of teacher training

afternoon, that apparently she had already been informed about—she had received a letter that she was supposed to pass on to her mum, but like most of those letters, she had forgotten.

So when the day hit, Mum, of course, was not there to pick her up.

So she was faced with a crossroads.

Walking home on her own.

Or letting reception know, so they could get in touch with Mum.

She was only about five at the time. So walking home wasn't really an option on her own.

But she certainly felt *capable* of walking home on her own.

She certainly felt like she knew her way back.

So she had taken off. On her own.

She had walked down roads that she thought she recognised.

And then cut through a park she thought she knew. Only she'd seen a few big, scary dogs up ahead, and suddenly she didn't really want to go that way, past them.

So she'd gone another way.

And it was not long after that, she realised she was lost.

The fear she felt. It was like the fear she felt when she was lost in the supermarket. Only worse. A whole lot worse.

Because she knew Mum wasn't in the building.

She knew she was nowhere around.

Nowhere nearby.

And that...

That was scary.

She kept walking, though. Crying. Some people stopped her. Tried to ask her if she was okay. But she didn't want to talk to them. They were scary. Mum always told her never to talk to strangers. But now, where she was, *everyone* was a stranger.

Eventually, someone must have reported her. Because the police showed up and told her they were going to take her home. She asked them if she was in trouble. They joked that she was, but then they took her home. And she thought Mum was going to be mad with her. But she wasn't. She just hugged her and told her never, ever to do that again.

And she didn't.

Until now.

She couldn't get over how quiet everything was. She had never really had the luxury of exploring this place. Even though she'd been trapped here for ages. But she got the sense that it used to be busier than this. More bustling than this.

As she walked, she saw these weird *patches* on the ground. They looked like puddles. Only thicker, somehow. Like puddles of glue. They gave off this weird smell, too. A smell she couldn't describe. That made her uneasy.

As she walked, she saw one or two people. One of them looked like a guard. Wearing the usual gear. The other was a woman. Didn't look like a captive. Just an ordinary woman.

But they seemed distracted. Once upon a time, she felt like walking around this place might've ended in her capture.

Now, it felt like it was everyone for themselves.

It didn't feel like there *was* any order anymore.

Like that *event*—whatever it was—had shattered everything.

She thought back to the event.

To the moment everything changed.

That blurry moment.

The moment she looked up at the sky and...

After that, blurriness.

It was dizzying. The whole thing. She kept forgetting why she was so exhausted. Why she was so worn out. Forgetting that she'd just been in captivity for God knows how long. Starved. Dehydrated. Been put right through the fucking wringer.

But she kept walking.

Towards the apartments Grace had told her about, right before she'd died.

It still stung. The memory of Grace's death. It sounded

absurd. Because before today, the thought of Grace's demise would have filled her with delight.

But when it actually happened—right before it happened—she had something of an epiphany.

Grace wasn't doing what she was doing for any other reason than wanting to protect her children.

And in those final moments, when it really came to it... she had sacrificed herself.

Could Georgia say she would have done the same thing if she had kids of her own?

Would she have taken a bullet for someone when her children's lives were at risk?

So she felt this need. To fulfil her promise to her. To find those children. To protect them. However she could.

She walked up to the apartment block. It looked pretty normal. Pretty ordinary. Red-bricked. About five storeys high.

And she didn't know whether she was going to find what she wanted to find in there.

She didn't know whether she was going to find the kids or not.

But she was going to try.

She was going to *have* to try.

She looked back over her shoulder.

Back down the road.

She saw people. Stumbling through the street.

She saw those weird patches on the road, under the brightness of the blue sky.

And, well into the distance, she saw Brian and Abigail and that girl, Ava, and the dogs.

She looked at them.

She felt that invisible thread connecting them.

Then, she swallowed a lump in her throat.

She turned around.

She stepped up to the apartment door.

And she walked inside.

She didn't know what she was walking into.

If she knew, she might have done things differently.

CHAPTER NINETEEN

Brian had almost lulled himself into something resembling a false sense of security when he heard the scream echoing from the apartments.

He had spent the last however long searching his immediate surroundings. These quiet streets. It really did feel like a ghost town. An empire, fallen.

It wasn't that it was *empty*. There were still a few people about, here and there. But there was no sense of order here anymore. No sense of structure. Even though he hadn't spent any real time in this place, that was the vibe he got. That it was ordered. Well-organised.

But now, it was just a disparate mix of parts. People, occasionally wandering around. Dogs. Making their way through these streets. Sniffing the ground. Wagging their tails.

There was no structure here anymore.

There was just...

The pieces of a former whole.

As he walked through these streets, another thought struck him. Was this confined to Galloway's safe zone? It couldn't be, could it? Because why *would* it be? That event. The event he had witnessed. It had to be wider than just this place. He wasn't sure why he was so certain. But that was just the feeling he got.

He looked up at the radio tower. Right beside him. Felt like he'd been searching for this thing forever. And now he'd got here, it wasn't what he was expecting to find. At all. He had been expecting a battle. Expecting a fight. A final stand.

In some ways, that was exactly what it had been.

But not for him.

He walked with Abigail right beside him. And Ava beside her. And the dogs. All closely behind. Another couple of dogs had joined them. One was called Wolf, apparently. Ava said he used to be Galloway's dog. And while Brian was reluctant to look after *anything* of Galloway's... a dog was different. Almost felt like he was reclaiming something, after what Galloway and his people did to Tabitha's dogs.

He looked at them all, and he wondered if this was a figment of his imagination. Abigail. His daughter. Ava. The girl he had pledged to save, all that time ago. He wanted to wrap them all in bubble wrap. He wanted to cling to them. He didn't want them to ever leave his sight again.

After the event, there was the question of what next. Where did they go from here? And in a sense... wasn't the answer to that question the same as it had always been?

They were going to have to find safety.

Safety, of some sort.

Wherever they may find it.

He realised, though, as he walked further through this abandoned town, that he was never going to be able to cling to them.

They were going to be tested.

They were all going to be tested again.

This wasn't going to be the end.

He heard the scream, and it cut through the silence. Echoed through it. And it woke him up to reality again. The reality that they weren't in some kind of dream world. That something very drastic had happened. Something truly horrendous. Something they still didn't truly understand.

He turned around. To the apartments. Where Georgia had headed towards a little while ago. It was Abigail who told him she'd gone that way. He wished she hadn't gone that way alone. They needed to stick together. They all needed to stick together.

And now, the first sense that her decision to go alone was the wrong one.

He looked at Abigail and Ava. Instinctively, a protectiveness washed over him.

"I'll go," he said. "You hold back."

But Abigail glared back at him.

And Ava did, too.

Both with that look in their eyes.

That look on their faces.

Like he was in no place to tell them what to do.

"I don't want—"

"We've spent a year surviving," Abigail said. "I've spent... I've spent all this time thinking you're dead. You're not... you're not stepping out of my sight, Dad. Ever again."

Hearing her speak like this... as much as Brian didn't want Abigail in any sort of danger, it was nice to hear her speak this way. There were so many things they had to discuss. Their distance. Their estrangement. The wrongs he'd made. And honestly, it felt like the time for that conversation would come. It would arrive. Soon enough.

But right now... right now, all that mattered was navigating their immediate situation.

And that started with the scream.

Georgia's scream?

That much was hard to tell.

But it certainly sounded that way.

He looked at Abigail.

He looked into her eyes.

He felt pain in his chest.

Pain, seeing how much older she was now.

Seeing how damned gorgeous she was.

He wanted to tell her to hold back.

He wanted to tell her that this was for him to investigate.

But in the end, seeing her, staring into his eyes… he realised that even though she was *his* little girl, she wasn't *a* little girl anymore.

And neither was Ava.

Both of them were here.

They were hardened.

And they were ready to face whatever they were about to face.

Together.

He looked at them.

Then at the dogs.

Then he looked around at the apartments, where the scream had come from.

He looked up at the sky.

Blue.

But greying.

Greying, ever so slightly.

Then, he swallowed a lump in his throat, and together with his daughter, together with the girl he had pledged to save… he ran.

CHAPTER TWENTY

Georgia stepped inside the apartment blocks, where she was hoping to find Theo and Elizabeth, and she immediately knew something was wrong.

The entrance area was empty. It looked like it had been quite a nice little reception area, once upon a time. There were quite a few apartments here. So it was probably quite a bustling little place.

It certainly wasn't busy or bustling anymore.

Two rifles were lying on the floor in the middle of this bright, airy entrance area.

Beside those rifles, Georgia saw two patches.

Two strange, gooey puddles.

They looked black on first inspection. But upon looking closer, Georgia realised they were actually translucent. Oily, almost. She didn't want to get too close to them. Not just because of that weirdly ominous smell coming from them. The smell of something both familiar and yet completely unfamiliar, simultaneously.

But she was beginning to get the sense that when the *event* happened—the event that turned night to day in a flash—these puddles were what was left of the people who had vanished.

She glanced down at these puddles in the entrance area as she walked past. She didn't want to stare at them for too long. It felt forbidden, somehow. Almost as risky as staring up at the sky, earlier.

When she looked down into these puddles, she didn't see her own face staring back at her.

She saw…

Nothing.

A void.

A total void.

And yet, the sense that something was down there.

Staring back up at her.

A sense she couldn't shake.

She walked through the entrance area and into the stairway. It was quiet in here, too. Sunny. Echoey. Dusty. There were a few more of these puddles. A few more of these patches. She tried not to focus on them. Even though it was pretty damned hard not to. Because it felt… otherworldly. A word she was trying not to consider or ponder too much. Because it scared her.

It was one thing to think they were dealing with some kind of virus. Some kind of infection.

It was another thing entirely to fear they were dealing with something…

Not of this world.

She climbed the staircase. Slowly. She felt far away from safety, now. Far away from Brian. From Abigail. From that girl, Ava. And from the dogs. She felt like she was in uncharted territory. Deep in uncharted territory.

But she just had to keep going.

She just had to keep climbing.

She had to find Theo and Elizabeth.

That was what she had pledged.

She climbed until she reached the floor Grace told her the kids were on. She stopped when she reached the door to that corridor. A real moment of hesitation, as she stood at that door.

The smell.

The same smell from those puddles.

So strong.

Her heart.

Racing.

Pounding.

She took a long, deep breath.

Even though she wasn't sure it was a good idea.

She swallowed a lump in her throat.

She had no idea what she was on the brink of discovering.

But she was about to find out.

She opened the door.

She expected to see something weird in this corridor. She wasn't sure what exactly. Just something... *different*.

But the corridor was completely normal.

Completely ordinary.

There were no signs of anything unusual at all.

And *that* was unusual in itself.

She walked down the corridor.

Slowly.

The floor creaking beneath every footstep.

She tried to calm herself. Tried to stop her heart from racing.

But she couldn't.

There was no stopping the fear, now.

She walked until she reached the room where Grace had told her she would find the kids when suddenly, a flash of *something* filled her mind.

It was hard to explain. Very hard to describe.

But she almost thought she was seeing *another* version of this reality.

Another corridor.

Only this corridor was filled with horrible, thick mushrooms, and strange bubbles were hovering through the air, hovering towards her, hovering…

And then she saw bodies.

She saw bodies.

Dangling from the ceilings.

Covered in vines.

Vines and mushrooms, and—

That substance.

That thick, black—no, *translucent*—substance.

She felt a sharp pain fill her forehead.

And before she could even make sense of any of it… she was back in the corridor again.

The walls were clear.

The whole damned corridor was clear.

And the door to this room was clear.

She gulped. What'd just happened… it didn't feel right. She had a headache. A tiny headache, right above her left eye now. She didn't think it was there before. She didn't know what was happening.

Only that it was probably in her head.

It was probably in her imagination.

She'd been through a lot. So it went without saying she was going to witness some shit.

Right?

She reached for the handle.

Heart racing now.

Trying to push aside that unsettling momentary experience.

A hallucination?

A dream?

She didn't know.

She couldn't know.

She stood at the door, and she thought of Grace.

That was what she had to focus on now.

That was all she *could* focus on.

The kids.

Finding them.

Helping them.

And then getting out of here.

She turned the handle.

Lowered it.

Pushed the door open.

Georgia was never one to scream.

But when she saw what she saw behind that door…

Nothing could stop her from screaming.

CHAPTER TWENTY-ONE

As they got closer to the building where the screaming came from, Ava noticed that weird feeling inside her body, getting stronger.

It was strange. It was hard to explain. It was like there was something *in* there. Moving around. Wriggling around, under her skin. No, not just under her skin. Deeper than that. Deep, deep under her skin. In her belly.

And it was wriggling around like it was trying to get out.

She looked up at the sky as she ran further towards the building. It wasn't as blue anymore. It looked... greyish. Like it was getting greyer, too. Like a storm was coming.

And Ava was worried about a storm coming. The last storm that came... that's when the *thing* happened. The thing that changed the night into day.

Maybe that's why Charlie was scared of storms. Maybe that explained it. Explained everything.

But she got this weird feeling that when the next storm came... something was going to happen.

Inside her.

She ran along with Brian. With Abigail. And with the dogs,

too. When she looked at the dogs, she noticed Doug and Ghost were both looking at her through the side of their eyes. They weren't looking closely at her anymore. It was as if they were scared of her. Like they were unsure of her.

Like they knew something about her that the other people here didn't.

Something about her that even *she* didn't.

She turned back around towards the apartment place where they were running when she saw something else.

It was weird. It was as if the daylight had gone again. Like it was nighttime again. Black. Pitch black.

And there were all these weird bubbles, hovering around everywhere, in the air.

Weird bubbles.

And weird mushroom things, growing up the sides of the buildings.

And...

She blinked a few times. To make sure she was seeing right.

And as she blinked... she noticed something weird.

Something she couldn't explain.

There were people.

People.

Rising up towards the sky.

People in helmets.

People with guns.

And normal people, too.

All rising right up towards the sky.

Being *lifted* up.

Lifted up by these long, black tentacles.

This long, stretchy black goo.

Towards...

She saw it. Up there. Up there in the sky above.

This *thing*.

It was almost impossible to explain.

Because it was unlike anything Ava had ever seen before.

It was in the sky. Only that maybe wasn't the best way of explaining it. It *was* the sky. Where the sky was—where the sky should be—there was just this *thing*.

People looked like they were rising up towards it. Like they were *falling* towards the sky.

Only...

No. That wasn't the case now.

They weren't falling to the sky anymore.

They were...

Frozen.

Completely frozen.

She looked up at this *thing* though. The thing where the sky used to be. As she looked closer at it... she realised she had seen it before. It was... it was like a ball. A massive ball.

Only it was opening up.

It was splitting right down the middle.

And as it split open, cracked open, black goo was oozing out of it, and...

She looked up towards it, and she wanted to look away.

But she could *feel* something.

Feel something inside her.

Moving up her belly.

Moving up towards her mouth.

Towards her throat.

Stinging the back of her throat, and...

Suddenly, she felt something tighten around her throat, and—

She was on the ground.

She was coughing.

She was spluttering.

She could taste blood.

Blood, and phlegm, and—

Burning.

Burning.

Right the way down her throat.

Right through her body.

Through all the muscles in her arms, and her legs, and her chest, and—

The sky.

She could only look up at the sky as she lay there on her back.

She lay there.

The dogs growling.

Barking.

One of them biting at her.

Then backing away.

And as they bit at her, she felt more pain.

She felt worse.

Even worse.

Something in her throat.

Something blocking her from breathing.

Something...

She looked up at the sky, and she thought of Mum again.

She thought of how she had found her.

She thought of the table she had been lying on.

She thought of the *thing* that came out of her.

And then, in a flash—in a horrible, momentary flash—Ava remembered.

Ava remembered exactly what had happened.

She felt that tightness around her throat.

She felt the pain in her body.

All the way through her body.

She felt the ringing in her ears.

And she tasted sick in her mouth.

And then, before she could think another thought...

A brightness filled Ava's eyes.

A warmth filled her body.

Then, nothing.

CHAPTER TWENTY-TWO

Brian wasn't exactly enamoured by the idea of running into that apartment and finding out who was screaming—and whether or not it was Georgia.

But he was even less enamoured by the idea of finding out exactly what was happening to Ava right now.

He didn't notice anything at first. Just this *sense*. You know how it can be. That sudden sense that something was *wrong*. That things weren't quite unfolding as you thought they would. As you expected them to.

But it was only when he looked back over his shoulder and saw Ava standing right there—still, completely still—and looking up at the sky, neck perfectly arched back, that he realised exactly what that unexpected development he was feeling uncertain about really was.

She was standing there. As described. Right in the middle of the road. She was looking up into the sky at something. Her eyes looked like they were turned right back. Into the back of her skull. But her body... her body was looking up at something.

At something above.

Right above.

And at that moment... suddenly, to Brian, nothing else mattered.

The scream from the apartments.

The fear of what might have happened to Georgia.

The uncanniness of everything around them.

Nothing else mattered.

All that mattered was Ava.

He ran back towards her. And as he did, he noticed blood.

Blood.

Trickling down her nostrils.

And a little out of her eyes, and her ears, too.

She was beginning to foam at the lips. Grow wobbly on her feet. Beginning to shake. To twitch.

And it was strange. Because as she twitched, and as she shook... Brian swore he felt the very day changing around him.

Like moments of night were creeping in.

She was on her tiptoes.

She was on her tiptoes, and those feet were shaking.

They were twitching.

It looked like something was lifting her up.

Lifting her up towards the sky.

Lifting her up towards...

He'd seen it.

He'd seen it, and suddenly it was appearing in his mind again.

The sky.

Opening up.

Opening up and threatening to drag him up there, like it dragged Galloway up there, and—

"Ava," he gasped.

He grabbed her. Even though he wasn't sure about it. Kind of like when someone epileptic was in the middle of a seizure. He didn't want to get this wrong. Didn't want to disturb her, if that might do her more damage.

But holding her... he realised she was covered in sweat. Dripping. Absolutely dripping.

And she was shaking hard, now.

Shaking hard, as she began to make this ghastly sound, from the very depths of her throat, and...

Her heart.

Her heart was beating fast.

So, so fast.

"What's happening to her?" Abigail asked.

Brian wished he could answer.

All he could do was hold Ava.

Hold her, and try his best to reassure her, as she continued to shake, and bleed, and...

"It's okay," he said. "I've got you. Everything's going to be okay."

He held on to her. As she started shaking. He looked up and saw Abigail. Looking at him. Then around, at the apartments. Right opposite. Towards where she'd heard that screaming coming from.

And then she looked back at Brian.

And at Ava.

The concern in her eyes.

Concern for Ava.

But also, a concern for whatever was going on in there, too.

And Brian didn't want to leave Ava. He didn't want to abandon her. He didn't want to abandon Abigail. That was the last thing he wanted to do. He wanted to stay with her. To keep her by his side. At all times.

But then...

Georgia.

He cared about Georgia, too.

He cared about *everyone*.

Before he could say another word, Abigail spoke.

"I can watch her," she said. "I can look after her. While you..."

And Brian shook his head. Because he didn't want that. He didn't want to leave her. Didn't want to leave them both together.

But at the same time...

He didn't want to leave Georgia, either.

Especially if she was in danger.

Especially if he could help.

If *someone* could help.

"I'm not going anywhere, Dad," Abigail said. Smiling at him a little. "I'm here. I'm right here. And I'm not going anywhere."

And he wanted to believe her. He wanted to believe she was telling the truth. That there was no word of a lie coming from her mouth.

But he knew damned well that promises like that couldn't be made in this world anymore.

He didn't want to leave Abigail. He didn't want to leave Ava. He didn't want to leave the dogs. It was one of his greatest fears.

But at the same time...

He knew what he *had* to do.

He looked at Abigail.

And at Ava. Still shaking. Still twitching. In her arms.

But calmer now, somehow.

Like those fits were settling down.

"I don't want to leave you," Brian said.

"And you won't be leaving us," Abigail said.

He looked at her. He wanted to argue. He wanted to stand his ground. He wanted to protest.

But then he thought about Georgia, in those apartments, and how she needed him right now.

"Look after her," Brian said. Leaning forward. Kissing her on her forehead. Hardly able to hold back his tears.

Abigail recoiled a little a first. Clearly uncomfortable with the physical contact. But then she seemed to settle. She seemed to allow it. "Look after yourself," she said.

He looked into her eyes. This moment. Stretching on forever.

"I love you," he said.

Abigail nodded. She opened her mouth. Paused. Hesitated. Then: "I... I love you too. Now go on..."

He looked at her.

At Ava.

Pale.

Bleeding.

Weak.

Then he looked around at the apartment where he'd heard the scream.

A scream that sounded very much like Georgia's.

He took a long, deep breath.

He swallowed a lump in his throat.

And then he ran towards those apartments.

Overhead, he swore he felt the blue sky beginning to darken...

CHAPTER TWENTY-THREE

Georgia could safely be described as "rather stoic."
She didn't like the idea of displaying emotions publicly. It was one of the reasons she thought George might've done the dirty on her, in the end. She was a little bit over the top when it came to expressing her love for him. Always wanting to hold his hand. Kissing him whenever they got tangled around a lamppost. Was she too emotional with him? Too lovey-dovey with him?

And when he'd leaked her photos and videos, she hated the idea of displaying any emotion or vulnerability publicly even more. Because the stuff in those videos. The intimacy. That was the ultimate lowering of her guard. The ultimate vulnerability.

And so many people had seen those photos. Those videos. She felt like they'd seen *her*. Her, without the mask on. The true, unfiltered her, that was supposed to be just for those closest to her. Not for the eyes of the world.

So after that ordeal, perhaps subconsciously, she had started to hide herself from the world, emotionally. Whereas at one time, she might've been expressive, *now*, she was anything but.

But when she opened the door and looked inside that apartment room... things changed.

Her old self crept through.

Which, considering all she had been through in captivity, said a lot about what she was looking at.

The first thing she noticed was the bed.

The sheets were white. And the bed was well made. Remarkably well-made. It almost looked unslept in. Untouched.

Except for the bloodstains.

All over the bed.

The blood looked thick. Honestly, the bed was absolutely drenched in it. It was as if it had been painted in it. Soaked in it. And then placed right back on the frame.

It smelled, too. Strong. Bitter. Metallic.

So red that it was almost black.

She heard a creak in the corridor, somewhere around her, and looked around. Conscious of that weird vision she'd had moments ago. But she couldn't see anything. No one was there.

Not that she could *see*.

But she was beginning to get the sense that what she *saw* wasn't the total picture.

She looked back around the room. Almost as if she was looking at an accident scene from the side of a road. Knowing deep down she shouldn't be looking.

But unable to turn herself away.

She stood at that door. Shaking. Heart thumping harder. Which she knew wasn't a good idea. If the infected were close... her fear would be enough to draw them right towards her. Like a beacon.

It didn't *feel* like the infected were close.

But that was part of the problem.

She sensed there was something in this room. Just around the corner. Just out of sight. She didn't want to peek her head around the door, though. Because she sensed that this was definitely going to be something she didn't want to see.

The room Theo and Elizabeth were in.

Grace's kids.

The blood. All over that double mattress.

This wasn't right.

She steadied herself. As well as she could. Knowing full well she was on the brink of seeing something she didn't want to see. Discovering something she didn't want to discover. Just *hoping* it wasn't what she thought it might be.

Grace's children.

The pledge she'd made.

The promise she'd made.

She would never forgive herself if she had failed them.

She knew she couldn't stand here forever, though.

Doing so was dangerous.

So she did what she knew she had to do right now.

She stepped further into this room.

She saw something, then.

In the corner of the room.

Against the wall.

Movement.

A glimpse of something...

Breathing?

Pulsating?

It was hard to make out at first.

Hard to tell.

But she got the sense she was on the brink of finding out exactly what it was.

She peeked around the corner of the room.

The smells growing stronger.

Her heart pounding harder.

And that's when she saw what she saw.

It took a few seconds to fully process what she was looking at.

It felt longer, though. Way, way longer. It was definitely a body of some form. Some kind of body, that was hard to explain. It was moving. Breathing. Pulsating.

But the closer she looked…

She realised it wasn't just any old "body" at all.

There was a little boy.

His arms were pinned to the wall.

Pinned to the wall by these weird, shroom-like vines.

His eyes were wide.

Green vomit and black goo were both seeping out of the corners of his mouth.

His tongue was dangling down his chin.

Moving around it.

Tentacle-like.

And there was something…

There was something *moving* around.

In his chest.

Inside him.

At first, Georgia thought it was his heart.

But it was moving too fast to be his heart.

Too hard.

It was…

Bobbing up and down.

Underneath his skin.

Trying to break out.

She stood there in the room. Frozen. Terrified. Unable to move. Barely even able to breathe.

Staring at this boy.

This poor boy.

Wanting to go over to him.

Wanting to help him.

But at the same time, unable to do a thing.

She felt frozen to the spot. But knowing she needed to get out of there.

When she saw the little black speck, right in front of her.//
She didn't know what it was at first. Not initially.

But the more she focused on it, the more it became clear.

It wasn't a floater in her eyes.

It was in front of her.

Dangling in front of her.

She saw this *thing* come into view.

And her heart started racing even harder.

Because this...

This was...

It was something dangling down in front of her.

Slimy.

Right before her eyes.

She looked at it, dripping from the ceiling like saliva.

Then she looked up at the ceiling.

Slowly.

She didn't want to.

But again, she didn't feel like she had a choice.

Like she had any control.

Any control at all.

When she looked up...

She saw her.

A little girl.

Only...

She was only *half* girl.

She had the face of a little girl.

But the body of something else.

Something dark.

Something slimy.

Something...

Unnatural.

The little girl's face stared down at her.

Pale.

Dead.

And then, it smiled.

Smiled, with these masses of long, sharp teeth.

And then, before Georgia could do a thing, she opened her mouth, and she ripped herself off the ceiling, and collapsed down towards Georgia.

Georgia screamed.

CHAPTER TWENTY-FOUR

Abigail held on to Ava and tried to ground herself in the moment as much as she possibly could.

But when a child looked to be dying, right beneath her—a child she had spent so long thinking about, consumed with guilt about these last few months—it was very hard not to get caught up in all kinds of thoughts.

She held Ava's back and her hand. Her hand was cold. So damned cold. Shaky, too. She held her like she'd wanted to hold her for all these days, weeks, and months since walking away from her. Since abandoning her. Leaving her. Something that still haunted her to this moment. Ava. Doug. She should never have done that. She was just... afraid. Afraid of something happening to her. And then losing her. And that being on her.

At that moment, she'd rather walk away than risk losing Ava.

Losing Doug.

That bond. That connection. It was dangerous. So dangerous. And that was why she had been so cold with her. Why she had been so critical. And distant, too.

She didn't want to soften Ava, for one.

But also, she didn't want to lose her.

And now she was here. Holding her hand. And somehow, Doug was here, too. And perhaps most bizarre of all, Dad was here. She'd spent so long here, captured by Galloway. And then in hiding, after escaping captivity. This had to be a dream. This had to be a figment of her imagination. It had to be some messed-up distortion of reality.

Especially after what happened to the sky.

The way it switched.

The way it changed.

Night to day. In an instant. In a flash.

It made Abigail shiver just thinking about it.

And so too did the thought of Dad, right now.

She looked up. Over at the apartment blocks. Where Dad had run to. In search of the scream. The one that sounded like Georgia. She didn't want Dad going in there. She didn't want to lose him. Not after so long.

But at the same time... she could see in his eyes what it meant to him.

Going in there.

Finding Georgia.

She needed to allow him to do that.

Even though it was clear neither of them wanted to lose each other again.

She stroked Ava's head. She had settled now. She felt cold, though. Cold, but clammy. Sweaty. She was breathing lightly. Gasping. Something had happened to her. Blood. From her nostrils. All over her face. And froth. In the corners of her mouth. She didn't look good. Didn't look well at all. Her skin had a greenish tinge to it.

But all Abigail could do was hold her.

Comfort her.

Pray.

She looked up at the dogs. All these damned dogs. They were settled here. But... they didn't seem comfortable around Ava, for some reason. They seemed unsure of her. And she could tell earlier that Ava felt odd about it, too. She'd picked up on it. Sensed something wasn't right.

And Abigail was trying to park those thoughts right now, as she held on to her.

But it was hard.

It was difficult.

It was...

She looked up, and she saw something in the distance.

It was hard to make out at first. But she could only best describe it as a sort of... a sort of shimmer. Like reality itself was shaking, somehow.

She squinted ahead. Looked closer at it. And she could see something in it, then. In this shimmer.

There were...

There were people inside it.

Figures.

And they were climbing out of it.

They were breaking through whatever it was.

They were...

She looked closer, and her heart began to race.

The dogs began to bark.

To whine.

Her stomach turned.

These figures.

They weren't people.

They were...

Suddenly, an urge.

To get inside.

To get away from here.

To get to Brian, and to get the hell away from this place.

She went to stand when suddenly, Ava tightened her grip around her hand.

She looked down.

Ava was staring up at her.

Her eyes were open.

But they were black.

Completely black.

She smiled.

Black ooze trickling out of every orifice.

She squeezed Abigail's hand tighter.

And then something shot out of her mouth—something long and tentacle-like—and towards Abigail's face.

CHAPTER TWENTY-FIVE

When Brian stepped inside the apartments, he began to regret it, right away.

He knew it was only natural. Abigail was outside. His daughter. A daughter he had spent so long hoping he would find again. Hoping he would be reunited with. She was outside. He'd left her out there. Because Ava wasn't well. Ava was sick.

Ava.

A girl he'd pledged to look after.

Pledged to protect.

She was outside, too.

He'd come in here because he'd heard Georgia. Screaming. He'd barely even had any chance to process the fact that *Georgia* was here, too. Georgia. The woman he'd travelled so far north with. Those long treks through the hills together. They'd formed a connection. A bond. And in the end... in the end, he'd *died* for that woman. Not quite literally, in the end. But he'd been on the brink of dying. Right on the brink.

And now *she* was here, too.

She was here, and she was in danger.

But there were still these mixed emotions. Mixed emotions about leaving Abigail and Ava out there. Was that the right thing to do? It *seemed* quiet out there. It *seemed* safe out there.

But that was part of *why* shit seemed so eerie. It might *seem* that way. But it *seemed* a bit *too* that way.

But, fuck. He'd made his decision now. He was in the apartments. Through the reception area. Up those creaky stairs.

And he was at the door leading to the corridor that Georgia was apparently heading towards, judging by her prints on the floor.

He stood at that door. To the corridor. He stood right outside it. And for some reason, he was hesitant. Nervous. Nervous about opening the door. There were lots of valid reasons. But there were quite a few reasons he couldn't put his finger on, too. Reasons he couldn't explain.

He got the sense that there was something behind these doors.

Something he didn't want to see.

It reminded him of his trip to Melbourne Terraces, what felt like forever ago. That trip to find Abigail. Those corridors. Those godawful corridors of that student apartment. His first true glimpse of the... hell, the *second form?* Was that the best thing to call it?

He got the feeling he was going to see something. When he pushed open those doors. That something was going to be waiting for him. Waiting for him in the corridor.

But at the same time... he was nervous.

Nervous about leaving Abigail and Ava out there on their own for too long.

So he put his hand on that door.

He held his breath.

He braced himself for whatever he was about to see behind that door.

Then, he exhaled, and he pushed that door open.

To his surprise—pleasant surprise—the corridor looked normal.

It was quiet. Empty. Eerie as fuck.

But there were no signs of shroom-like growths on the ceilings.

No signs of mummified bodies.

Dripping that steaming black tar.

Just an ordinary, empty corridor.

Only that momentary delusion of normality soon changed.

When he saw the door.

Ajar.

And the blood.

The blood, seeping out of it.

He stood there. Heart racing. Faster and faster.

He tried to keep his calm.

Keep his cool.

But his mind was doing somersaults.

Jumping to all kinds of conclusions.

Georgia.

She was screaming because she was in danger.

She was screaming because she'd been attacked.

She was screaming because...

No.

No, he needed to push those thoughts aside.

He needed to push them aside, and focus on what was in front of him.

Only on what was in front of him.

He walked into the corridor.

Closer to that room.

To that open door.

Trying to tell himself that it wasn't necessarily Georgia.

It could be someone else.

She wasn't the only person in here.

There had to be *more*.

He stepped closer to that door. Head spinning even more. Feeling like he was in a daze. In a dream. A bad dream. A nightmare.

He got to the edge of the door.

He stood there.

For a second.

For a long, drawn-out second.

He tried to breathe in.

Tried to inhale.

Tried to let the fear go.

He had to brace himself.

He had to be ready.

He had to prepare.

He swallowed a lump in his throat, and he stepped towards the door.

Just before he did, he heard something.

Rustling.

Creaking.

To his left.

He looked around.

He didn't see anything.

Any movement.

Anything at all.

He gulped again. His jaw was clenched. Really clenched. He made a conscious effort to loosen it. One of Kelly's old instructions. Didn't want him grinding his teeth anymore. Clenching them in the night.

He loosened his jaw, and he turned around to that room.

The one with the blood inside.

Almost immediately, he clenched his jaw again.

There wasn't just blood on the carpet.

There was blood *everywhere*.

On the bed.

On the walls.

It was a bloodbath in here.

He stood there. His heart racing even more. Thumping.

He got the sense that something was moving.

Something moving, in the corner of that room.

In the corner of his eye.

He took a step.

A long, slow step.

Inside the room.

Not a lot.

But enough.

Just enough.

He stepped inside the room enough that he could see.

That he could see what that movement was.

Even though he wasn't sure he wanted to.

Even though he was afraid of it.

He stepped inside the room, and then...

Something was lying on the floor of the room.

Two bodies.

Two broken, twisted bodies.

He felt sick upon seeing them.

Tasted sick.

Almost vomited.

Almost threw up.

Because there was a third body.

A third body that he recognised.

A hole in her back.

And something...

Something had *climbed* out of her back.

And something was sitting on top of her, now.

Chewing the flesh of the dead bodies in the room.

Brian stood there, and he could only stare.

He could only stare at the scene in front of him.

At the three bodies.

Two children.

And one…
One older.
A woman.
A woman he recognised.
Lying flat on her stomach.
Her neck twisted.
Her face pale.
Drained of blood.
Greyed-out eyes.
"Georgia," he whispered.
And then, he saw the body above her.
The figure.
Long-limbed.
Slender.
Shiny.
Dark. But with an almost oily translucence.
He looked at that being.
Perched there.
Chewing raw flesh.
And he knew he needed to step away.
He needed to walk.
But before he could move…
That figure started turning around.
Turning at the neck.
Twisting.
Twisting right around, without its body twisting.
And when Brian saw what was looking at him—staring at him—there was nothing he could do to suppress his fear.
A face.
A face was staring at him.
A face he recognised.
Georgia's face.
Georgia's face, plastered to this…
This *thing*.

It looked at Brian.

Looked right into its eyes, with its dead eyes.

Blood trickling down its chin.

Body shimmering.

And then, as Brian stood there, it stood up.

Climbed to its feet.

Towered above Brian.

Brian could only stand there.

He could only watch.

But there was one thing for sure.

He needed to get out of this room.

He needed to get out of this place.

He needed to—

That's when the figure opened its mouth, and let out a blood-curdling scream.

CHAPTER TWENTY-SIX

When Abigail saw the weird, long black tentacle bursting out of Ava's throat, she was pretty fucking sure she *had* to be hallucinating.

But she didn't take much time to think about it. She couldn't afford to.

Because it was shooting right towards her.

She rolled out of the way almost immediately. Honestly, she was pretty impressed with her own reactions. Her own reflexes.

Rolling onto her side.

Out of the way.

She landed on her back with a heavy thud. Cracked her head in the process. Bit her tongue, too. Which tasted pretty rough. Metallic. Like blood.

She lay there, heart racing. The dogs barking a little. But whining, too. They weren't happy. They weren't happy one bit.

And as Abigail lay there on her back... she could not quite comprehend what she was witnessing.

What she was looking at.

Something was *climbing* out of Ava's mouth.

Physically clambering its way out of her mouth.

Her eyes were rolled back.

Her cheeks were splitting.

The corners of her mouth, cracking apart.

She was shaking profusely, as she vomited, and choked, and gasped, and gargled, and as this *thing*—this entity—ripped itself out through her throat.

And all the while... Abigail could see something else.

In the distance.

That shimmer.

And figures ripping their way through it.

Breaking their way through that shimmer, almost as if they were ripping out of another reality itself, and into this one.

She lay there on the ground. Staring at the figures in the distance. Still hard to make out. But getting closer. Closing in.

And then she looked at Ava.

This *thing*.

Still clambering its way out of her mouth.

Like it didn't want to be inside her.

Like...

It climbed out of her.

Ava was pale.

Completely pale.

She looked around.

Vomit oozing down her chin.

Eyes completely bloodshot.

Burst blood vessels.

But she looked *alive*.

She didn't have that same glassy-eyed emptiness the infected had.

She looked *alive*.

But then... she collapsed to the road with a thud.

A horrid thud.

Abigail's heart raced. She could see more of these things, now. These figures. She could hear screaming again. Gunfire. Something was happening. The bright blue sky. It was turning greyer. It was cracking. Breaking.

The weird peace they'd enjoyed... that was all falling apart.

It was all collapsing.

And in its place... chaos was resuming.

She heard something, then.

Thudding.

Things thudding down from...

From *above*.

And she noticed something, too.

The grey skies above.

Sudden grey skies.

That shimmer.

And that rain.

That jet-black rain.

She blinked a few times. She couldn't believe what she was seeing. What she was witnessing. There was almost a familiarity to it. Almost a sense that she had seen it before. Maybe in a dream. It was hard to say.

One way or another, reality was being shattered.

Shattered to pieces.

She couldn't pretend to understand what was happening.

But she didn't really have the time to contemplate it right now.

She barely had the time to contemplate the figures, staggering her way.

Not gasping.

Snarling.

Groaning.

Just...

Walking.

She didn't even have the time to focus on Ava.

Or the dogs.

Whining.

Hairs on their backs, right on end.

All she could focus on was this figure.

It seemed to be growing. Right in front of her.

Forming.

Right before her eyes.

Slimy, dark skin.

Insect-like.

Covered in translucent goo.

Wet, slurping sounds, as it unfurled.

It stood tall. Seven and a half feet at least. And it looked *almost* humanoid.

Almost.

But more like a caricature of a human.

Like an *impression* of a human. Drawn by someone who had only ever seen one human before. In the darkness. While squinting.

Long arms.

Muscular.

Long legs.

But the most striking thing of all?

Its...

Its face.

It was the face of a woman.

Staring down at her.

Looking at her with wide eyes.

Almost smiling.

Almost.

It looked at her. Honestly, though, this unknown woman's face just seemed *borrowed* rather than real. It looked drawn-on.

Until it opened its mouth, which wasn't *quite* where her mouth was—it was more like a split, a crack, right down the middle.

And out of that mouth...

A long, black tongue.

Sharp teeth.

Abigail sat there as these other figures inched closer.

As *this* figure just looked down at her.

Not making a noise.

More like it was watching her.

Studying her.

Waiting for her to make her move.

She glanced down at Ava.

She noticed the figure look down at Ava, too.

Almost as if it was sensing her intentions.

The dogs, all growling, all around it.

Her heart started beating faster.

Even though she needed to keep her cool.

She needed to get to Ava.

And she needed to get her to safety.

She needed to do it now.

She gulped.

She looked back up at this *being*.

At the rest of the figures.

Walking closer.

And as they got closer, she realised they *all* had these weird faces.

These weird, drawn-on faces.

Like artists' impressions of people.

Inching towards her.

She looked back down at Ava.

She gritted her teeth.

She held her breath.

That urge.

That need.

That need to get inside.

That need to hide.

She had to time this right.

She knew what she had to do.

She reached for Ava, suddenly.

Quickly.

She grabbed her.

She went to pick her up.

But before she could grab her, before she could drag her away…

The entity grabbed Abigail's arm.

Grabbed it, with its cold, slimy imitation of a hand.

A bright, piercing light filled her eyes.

A warmth filled her body.

And then…

Silence.

CHAPTER TWENTY-SEVEN

Brian thought he knew fear at this point.

Truth be told, he thought he knew fear *before* the outbreak. He'd been in his fair share of hairy situations both in the police and out of work. Walking through seemingly abandoned houses, just waiting for someone with a knife to leap out. Or the car accident, when he was a child. The airbags, all inflating, all around him, and suffocating him, and...

Yeah. Just thinking about it now was enough to send a shiver down his spine.

He thought he knew fear from his experiences in the outbreak, too. Again, he'd had more than his fair share of fear-inducing moments. Run-ins with the infected. Run-ins with dodgy people. Run-ins with... well, things he didn't quite understand.

But for some reason—perhaps it was a combination of the fact that he'd just found his daughter, and that Ava was here, too, and in danger, and the dogs were outside, and...

Georgia.

Georgia's face.

Georgia's twisted, contorted face, on this *thing*.

He looked at it.

He looked into her eyes.

Only they weren't *her* eyes.

They were pale imitations of her eyes.

Maybe it was a combination of all these things. And the sense of the unknown.

But Brian wasn't sure he had ever experienced fear like the fear he was experiencing right now.

And it didn't get any better, either.

Because that's when he heard something.

Down the long corridor of this apartment block.

He didn't want to turn around. He didn't want to look. He didn't want to turn his attention from the being with Georgia's face for a single moment.

But sometimes, instinct just took hold, didn't it?

Sometimes, regardless of your best efforts, and your best intentions... you can't control your actions.

So he turned his head.

He looked down the corridor.

Towards that *sound*.

As he turned, he realised it sounded like... like some kind of tapping. Like nails on a chalkboard. Tapping against it.

He couldn't shake the fear inside him. That thick cloud of fear. Building inside him. Even though he knew it wasn't a good thing. Even though he knew it was something he needed to allow. Something he couldn't experience any resistance to.

Despite all these things... he couldn't shake the fear.

Especially when he saw what he saw.

There was a dark figure.

Clinging to the side of the wall, right beside another door, further down the corridor.

It was literally clinging to the wall. Like some sort of reptile. First thing that came to mind for Brian was a gecko, on holiday. Gripping to the wall.

Still.

Very still.

It had this oily, translucent skin. And it was staring at Brian with these eyes. Black eyes. A face underneath it. Greyish skin. Not quite human.

It was just…

Clinging there.

It was just dangling from that wall.

Staring at him.

And the creepiest thing about it?

It didn't look threatening. It didn't look *anything*.

Just this blank face.

This blank face.

Glaring at him.

Studying him.

And then this being started shifting towards him.

His heart thudded faster.

He heard more noises.

More sounds.

Sounds like…

Cracking.

Splitting.

Like the very fabric of space and time was crumbling before his eyes.

He heard something else, then.

Something that gave him the biggest fright of all.

A gasping noise.

From the one in front of him.

From the one like *Georgia*.

He turned back around and looked at her.

Her head had extended from her neck.

Underneath that head—that *face*—long, stringy, black veins.

All holding it together.

Brian could only stand there.

He could only stand there, even though he didn't want to.

Because there was only one thing he wanted.

There was only one thing he needed right now.

To get the hell out of this place.

He knew he needed to keep his cool. He knew he needed to be careful where fear was concerned.

But there was nothing he could do right now.

He turned around, and he ran.

He ran down the corridor as fast as he fucking could.

He felt like he could hear footsteps.

Thumping towards him.

Shrieks.

Shrieks, and noises he had never heard before.

Echoing around this corridor.

Inching closer.

But he just kept on going.

He kept on going, even though he started to wonder whether he should have stood his ground.

Stood his ground, like someone trapped in a forest and faced with a bear. That's what they always say, isn't it? Stand your ground. Stand up for yourself. Stand tall.

And in theory, that's all good and well.

But in practice...

Yeah.

Not so fucking easy.

He ran.

Down the corridor.

Towards the door.

Heart racing.

Chest tightening.

Trying to get a grip.

Trying to get a hold of his fear.

Trying not to lose control.

He reached the first door at the end of the corridor.

Barged through it.

Reached the staircase.

He swore he could see things in the corners of his eyes.

Getting closer to him.

Approaching him.

Closing in on him.

But he just ran.

He just ran, down those stairs.

Further down those stairs, and...

He lost his footing.

Right by the bottom of the steps.

He tumbled over.

Rolled over.

Collided with the steps, and then the floor, and then tasted blood, and...

He lay on his back.

His head spinning.

His vision blurry.

Looking up at those top steps.

Waiting for them to open.

He thought of Abigail.

Of Ava.

Of the dogs.

He thought of them out there, and how he needed to get out there.

How nothing else mattered.

Not anymore.

He pushed himself to his feet.

As hard as he could.

Even though his head was aching.

Even though his whole damned *world* was spinning.

And he staggered through the reception area.

Towards the door.

Away from these apartments.

Away from...

Georgia.

Shit.

Georgia.

He'd seen her. Seen what had happened to her. What the infected—or whatever these things were—had done to her.

He swallowed a lump in his throat.

So long waiting for a reunion.

And... snuffed out.

Just like that.

He ran through the reception area, towards the door, and he noticed that the reception seemed to have changed, all around him.

There were things on the walls.

Mould.

Mushrooms.

And a smell in the air.

A horrible, musty smell.

"Keep going," he muttered. "Keep going..."

He limped a little further, the urgency all too much for him now.

And then, he slammed against the front door.

The doors opened up.

Right in front of him.

He tasted the air.

The freshness of the air.

A moment's relief.

A moment where everything was okay again.

And then...

When he saw what was ahead of him, the urgency of his situation dawned on him, all over again.

CHAPTER TWENTY-EIGHT

Abigail had experienced some weird shit in her life.
But nothing quite compared to the weirdness she was experiencing right now.

Her vision started flashing. Lights, surrounding her. Getting closer to her. They were strange colours, too. Colours she hadn't seen before. Colours she couldn't identify even if she was asked to.

And even though she knew she was afraid, at some instinctive level, these colours and these visions were all rather beautiful.

As were the sounds.

The sounds were just as indescribable as the visions in front of her. Just as impossible to comprehend. They were sweet, somehow. The sweetest song. Only... there was an alien quality to them. Beyond her comprehension. Like something she couldn't quite put her finger on.

There were these familiar smells, too. Baked bread, just like Mum used to make it. The smell of Dad's deodorant, before he went to work. The smells of candy floss, and the taste of it, and its softness, deep in her mouth.

And all these sensory experiences made her feel *warm*.

They made her feel secure.

Made her feel safe.

Even though there was this deep, instinctive feeling that she should feel anything but.

She wanted to think about *why* things felt so unusual, logically.

But at this moment, it was a *feeling* that took over.

It was a *feeling* that she couldn't look beyond.

A feeling she couldn't get past.

There was this sense, deep within, that something was *holding* her.

That something was *happening* to her.

That something was holding her arm, and it was getting closer to her.

Getting closer to her memories, to what made her *her*, and...

And before she could even grow fearful of the prospect, she was in her memories again.

But this one wasn't a good memory.

She was in her kitchen.

Mum and Dad were arguing.

Mum was shouting, really loud.

And Dad was just sitting there, getting redder and redder, and...

And then Mum said something she didn't understand, something about someone at work, and how they'd told Dad he should speak to someone, about something that happened at *his* work, and...

And then Dad flipped.

He threw the plate across the room.

And even though Abigail didn't think he *meant* to throw it at her, it hit her.

It hit her, and it smashed against her face, and...

Dad came over. He was so sorry. And he looked sorry, too.

Mum was holding her. Telling her everything was going to be okay. But that they needed to get out of here. Needed to go.

And even though Dad was saying sorry, and *kept* saying sorry, and had gone pale, really pale… she felt scared of him from that day.

She had to see him quite a lot, even though he didn't live with them anymore. And he tried. But no matter how long Abigail spent with him, she couldn't forget the kitchen. The plate. Thrown. Right across the room.

How scared she'd felt.

Someone she thought cared for her. Cared about her.

Scaring her.

When she got older, she didn't see Dad as much. She didn't want to. It wasn't that she didn't love him. She could just never see him the same again. He always had that look in his eyes. Like he was haunted. Haunted by what had happened, all those years ago.

But when she'd seen him again, here, in this place… somehow, everything had been different. Very, very different.

She'd forgotten the past.

She'd forgotten every bit of it.

And all she had seen was Dad.

She felt these memories flooding back in.

Warmer memories, now.

Times with Dad where she *wasn't* scared.

Times with Dad where he *didn't* feel guilty.

She thought about all these times, and she felt the *thing* tightening around her arm, as *something* got closer to her, and…

"Abigail!"

A voice.

Shouting.

Shouting, from somewhere far away.

Like it was miles away.

A voice that sounded like *Dad's*.

"Abigail! Wake up! Wake…"
She heard that voice.
She heard it getting closer.
She heard…
The singing.
The warmth.
And then…
Nothing.

CHAPTER TWENTY-NINE

When Brian stepped out of the apartment building, of all the sights he could possibly have seen, he couldn't think of any worse than the one in front of him.

Ava was on her back. Lying flat. Still.

The dogs were all around. Barking.

But the hairs on their backs were raised.

And in the distance...

Something was coming.

The air looked like it was shimmering, somehow. It was impossible to explain any other way. The closest thing Brian could think of was the surface of a bubble. That sort of pinkish, bluish, hard-to-identify glow.

It was just like there was a bubble there.

And that bubble was being pierced.

And out of that bubble...

Figures.

Figures like the one that ripped itself out of Georgia's body.

Figures like the ones in the apartment blocks.

All running this way.

All moving this way.

All getting closer.

And all of that was terrifying. None of that was good. Went without saying.

But nothing was quite as terrifying as what was happening with his daughter.

There was something by Ava's side.

And truth be told, judging by how wide Ava's mouth was, it looked like it had climbed its way out of her body.

Dragged its way out, leaving that residue trickling down the corners of her mouth.

And it was standing over Abigail, now.

It was standing over his daughter.

It was standing over her, and...

It was holding her arm.

It was holding her arm, tight.

And it was inching towards her mouth.

It was getting closer to her mouth.

Black tendrils inching towards her mouth, and her nostrils, and her ears, and her face, and...

He couldn't think.

He couldn't *anything*.

He could only run towards his daughter.

Run towards Abigail.

As fast as he fucking could.

He ran. And as he ran, he swore he heard movement behind him. He swore he heard the apartment doors, creaking open. He swore he heard popping. Weird popping sounds, filling the sky.

But he could only run.

He could only run towards Abigail.

Run towards his daughter.

Run towards...

This *thing*.

It looked like it had Ava's face.

And judging by what had just happened to Georgia...

That wasn't good news.

That wasn't fucking good news at all.

Because it meant Ava was...

No.

No, he couldn't think like that.

Not now.

He just had to get to Abigail.

He just had to get to his daughter.

He just had to do everything he could.

He shouted.

Screamed her name.

Tried to get her to wake.

Tried to break her free of whatever trance she was in.

And it reminded him of something, now.

Seeing her like this.

He'd seen this in someone before.

Earlier on.

When the infected were close. This trance-like state. Inducing a weird mishmash of senses.

He'd seen it, and it was as if it was getting stronger.

It was getting more intense.

It was changing.

It was...

"Abigail!" he screamed.

He saw something, then.

She turned around.

She looked right at him.

And her eyes.

Her eyes looked like they were rolling back.

Like they were rolling back in her skull, and...

And then he saw the *being*.

Right beside her.

Looking at him now.

Looking at him with this curiosity, as he hurtled towards it.

And even though he was afraid... even though he was completely fucking terrified—not for himself, but for his daughter—he ran towards it, and he braced himself to throw himself at it, and...

Suddenly, a flash.

A vision.

A dark vision, filling his mind.

It was night again.

It was night, and there were bodies, floating.

Floating everywhere.

Floating midway between the ground and the sky.

And above...

In the *sky*.

It wasn't the sky.

It was this... this shimmer.

This bubble-like shimmer, right above.

With little holes in it.

Little, popping holes, and...

And then a pain.

A pain in the middle of his chest.

A pain that reminded him of when he'd stepped on a jellyfish in Greece.

Only that was on the bottom of his foot.

Whereas this... this was in the middle of his chest.

Right in the middle of his chest, and...

And then it was light again.

He was here.

He was opposite his daughter.

He was opposite Abigail.

She was looking at him.

She was looking right at him.

Right into his eyes.

And he was looking at her, too.

He could feel it.

This was real.

This was all real.

This was...

And then he looked into her eyes, and he noticed something else.

He looked into her eyes, and he noticed a pain in her eyes.

He noticed *shock* in her eyes.

He looked into her eyes, and he noticed that she was looking *down*.

At his...

At his chest.

He looked down.

Slowly.

Even though he didn't want to.

Even though he couldn't even bear to.

He looked down.

Lowered his head.

Slowly.

That pain.

That pain he'd felt when he was having the vision.

Here again.

Right here.

Right...

When he looked down, and when he saw it, he almost didn't believe what he was seeing.

Not at first.

But when he looked closer, and when he saw it...

It made sense.

It all made a complete, total sense.

There was a long, sharp, black *thing* piercing through the middle of his chest.

Right through the middle of it.

And out through his back, too.

And it was coming from the being with Ava's face.

CHAPTER THIRTY

Abigail snapped out of her trance to the sight of her dad being impaled right in front of her.

He was just inches away from her. Looking at her. Wide-eyed. Like that first memory she had of him. Zooming her across the room, like an airplane. Holding her high, high above everything, so that the world looked so far down beneath her—the world of the carpet.

And she couldn't stop laughing. She couldn't stop laughing, and neither could he. She remembered that well. Might be one of her first memories. But it was one of her clearest.

The smell of the air freshener that took her back to childhood, whenever she smelled it.

The taste of porridge on her lips.

And Dad's big, warm hands, as he whizzed her around the room.

Those big, smiling eyes.

Back when he was happy.

Back before everything went so wrong.

She saw those eyes staring at her right now, and time stood still.

The entity. The one that had ripped itself out of Ava's mouth. Then grabbed her and made her start hallucinating. Witnessing shit. Weird as fuck shit.

Its arm—if it could be called an arm—had extended out of the being that had ripped itself out of Ava's mouth.

It had sharpened, by the looks of things.

And it was now sticking through the middle of Dad's chest.

Dad's eyes were wider now. Time stood still. She had this instinct. This urge. To scream. But at the same time, she couldn't. She just couldn't. She couldn't make a single noise. A single sound.

She could only stand there.

She could only look at Dad.

Into those wide eyes.

Behind, she heard footsteps approaching.

And ahead, too. The apartments. The ones he'd come from.

She saw movement there, too.

Inching towards the windows in there.

Then towards the doors.

But everything just stood still for her at that moment.

The being.

Its extended arm, ripping through his chest.

And that humming noise.

That low, eerie humming noise, seeping out of the mouth of this thing—or more out of its entire body.

Dad stood there. He opened his mouth to speak. A little blood came out. Trickled down his chin.

And she wanted to grab that arm.

She wanted to rip it out of him.

She wanted to drag it out of him, and then get him help, and then—

"Take her," Dad gasped. "Take her and go. Take her and..."

She shook her head. She couldn't speak. If she tried to speak, she would cry.

But she could see from the look in Dad's eyes what he wanted.

She could see what he was asking her.

"I love you," he gasped. With those haunted eyes. "Always... always loved you. And I'm sorry. I'm so sorry I was..."

He trailed off. He coughed. This beast—this entity—still standing there.

Long arm still piercing through his chest.

"Loved you. Always. Always. My girl. My girl..."

And Abigail wanted to step up to him.

She wanted to hug him.

She wanted to hold him tight and tell him everything was going to be okay.

But at the same time...

She couldn't even get near to him.

The blade-like arm through his chest.

And the knowledge that if she came into contact with him, she might start seeing the visions she had seen before, and next time, she wasn't sure she would be able to get out of them.

He looked at her with sad eyes.

He looked at her with a smile.

"I love you," he said. "I..."

She gulped.

She swallowed a lump in her throat.

The footsteps getting closer.

Everything closing in on her.

"I love you too, Dad," she said. "I always loved you. Every single day. I'm sorry... I'm sorry too."

She could barely keep it together now.

Barely hold it all together.

But she had to.

She had to.

Dad looked into her eyes.

He smiled at her.

"Look," he said. Staring off into the distance. Beyond her.

"Mum... Mum is here. I have to... I have to go to her now. I have to..."

She looked into his eyes, and she didn't see sadness anymore.

She saw happiness.

Happiness, glowing right across his face.

She sensed the figures getting closer.

Closer, from all directions.

She heard screams in the distance.

She heard gunshots again.

She heard...

Footsteps.

She looked into Dad's happy eyes.

And as much as she wanted to hold him, as much as she wanted to pull him close, as much as she wanted to tell him everything was going to be okay, and that she was here now...

She turned around.

She grabbed Ava's limp body.

And, with the dogs beside her, she ran away.

CHAPTER THIRTY-ONE

Brian watched Abigail, Ava, and the dogs disappearing into the distance, and even though a part of him knew he should feel sadness... he felt nothing but happiness.

Nothing but warmth.

Because, deep down, he was so, so sure that they were going to be okay.

He watched them running off into the distance. There was a brightness beyond them. Like a rising sun. Or was it a setting sun? It was hard to tell. Whatever it was, it was beautiful. The most beautiful sunrise or sunset he had ever seen.

And he'd seen some beautiful sunsets in his life. Some beautiful sunrises. With Sue. With Abigail. With Kelly. Sunrises when driving home from a long night shift at work. Sunsets on holidays, to France, and Spain. Or just in the British countryside, camping with Kelly.

These were the memories he found racing to him right now. The memories he found flooding in. Filling his body with warmth.

Even though he was well aware something was piercing right through the middle of his chest.

And even though he was well aware that Abigail, Ava, and the dogs were running away.

Because they had to.

He watched Abigail running off into the distance. Ava in her arms. The dogs by her side. And this confidence returned again. This assuredness. This certainty that they were going to be okay. They were all going to be okay.

Because they were strong.

They were so, so strong.

His ears were ringing. He could hear something else, too. A humming noise. It was unfamiliar. But it was actually rather beautiful. It soothed him. It reminded him of being a child. In his mother's arms. Her laughter. Dad's whistling—always whistling.

It gave him that same feeling.

That same sense.

There was a familiar smell, too, and a comforting quality to it. It reminded him of different things. Of bread, baking. Of sunscreen. Of wood, crackling on an open fireplace. Of Christmas dinner.

All these smells, all these memories, all merging together, welding together, in the most beautiful combination.

Sights.

Sounds.

Smells.

Tastes.

And even the sense of touch, too.

All of them.

Merging together.

Combining.

But he didn't want to resist this movement. Not anymore.

He wanted to allow it.

He wanted to fall even further into it.

Because it was too nice to turn away from.

He saw the eyes of the creature staring at him, then.

He saw it in detail.

That oily skin. Moving, somehow. As if it was made up of a load of smaller parts, all merging together.

He saw that face. An unfamiliar face. The face of a woman. An older woman who reminded him of Ava, somehow.

Staring at him.

But her eyes didn't look empty anymore.

Her eyes didn't look dead.

They looked…

Sad.

Genuinely sad.

He looked into those eyes, and even though this thing was alien to him—so, so alien—he wasn't afraid of it. Not anymore.

Because, looking into its eyes… he realised there was nothing to fear.

There was nothing to fear at all.

He looked up at it, and he felt like he understood, all of a sudden.

He felt like he understood its motives.

He felt like he understood why it was doing what it was doing.

He felt he understood everything, at a deeper, subconscious level.

And as he stood there, he felt like his memories were becoming the memories of this being, and they were merging, they were mixing together, and…

"We just want to remember, too," a voice said. From somewhere within. But not really in words. More… spoken *inside* him. Like it was in his own head.

"We just want to live, too. We want to be able to remember. Memory isn't something we have. Memory is something so few have. But you can remember. We want that. That's why we need you…"

He looked up at this creature.

He looked up at this being.

He looked right up, into its eyes.

And then he looked above it.

At the sky.

The bright, beautiful, shimmering sky.

He looked up there, and he saw Abigail up there.

Ava up there.

The dogs up there.

Kelly.

And Sue.

He saw them all looking down at him.

He saw them all smiling at him.

And, as a warm tear streamed down his cheek, he smiled too.

"I'm coming home," he said. "I'm... I'm ready now."

The creature stroked his face. That's what it felt like. As if it was comforting him. Learning what "comforting" was.

And then, as a warmth filled his body even more, he lifted up, towards the sky.

Towards the brightness.

Home.

CHAPTER THIRTY-TWO

Abigail didn't stop running until she was absolutely sure she was miles from the place.

And when she finally got far enough away, even *that* didn't feel far away enough.

But she couldn't stop her shaking knees from collapsing to the ground.

It was raining now. The blue skies had disappeared pretty quickly. It kind of felt like she'd left that nice weather behind, in the safe zone. *Safe zone.* What a piss-take. Felt like some kind of sick joke even *thinking* about it that way.

She was in an overgrown area off the main streets. An old public footpath. Then up some foliage, by the side of a railway bridge. Her legs were sore. Her arms were sore. Her entire body was sore. She had spent so long trapped in that place that doing any sort of movement for any extended period was a challenge.

Not to mention the fact that she had been carrying Ava, too.

Ava lay on the ground beneath her. Her heart was still beating. Lightly. She was breathing, too. Only a little bit.

But she was still alive.

She was still alive, and so she couldn't just leave her there.

Even after what she'd witnessed.

The corners of her mouth looked like they had been split a little bit at the edges. Bleeding. The black goo had mostly disappeared now. Just blood. Blood, and scabbing.

Abigail wasn't sure how she felt about taking Ava out of that place. Because it felt like that place was cursed. Rotten. To the core.

But at the same time... she thought of Dad, and her stomach sank.

She was trying not to think about what had happened to Dad. What she'd witnessed. Finding him. The elation she'd felt. The sense that they had so many years to make up for.

And then...

And then just losing him.

Losing him, just like that.

Watching that *being* stick a long, sharpened blade made from its own form, right through the middle of him.

Seeing him smile.

Hearing him tell her to run away.

And to take Ava.

To take the dogs.

Not wanting to go.

Not wanting to leave his side.

And then realising that she had to.

Because if she didn't try to get away—try to take Ava and the dogs away—then they were all going to die, too.

For nothing.

She knelt there. Ava lying unconscious underneath her. Breathing ever so lightly. The dogs were all sitting around, too. Happy enough. But clearly exhausted, too. Clearly feeling the weight of all that had happened. She didn't even know their names, other than Doug. The others: A St Bernard dog. A little yappy type. A couple of husky-type dogs. At least that's what she thought they were, anyway.

She sat there with these dogs all around her and Ava—a circle around them both, like they were trying to protect them.

And she wasn't sure what to do. She wasn't sure what to think. Her mind kept wandering to Dad.

To his eyes.

His kind eyes.

Their moment of reunion.

And then…

No.

She bit her lip. Hard. So hard she tasted blood.

She squeezed her eyes shut.

Hoping it would make the images go away.

But if anything, it just made those images even worse.

Even stronger.

Even more powerful.

She opened her eyes. Her ears were ringing. Her eyes were stinging. The air was cold. It was grey. Really grey. Above, she heard thunder. Rumbling closer. Rain. Cold rain, falling heavily from above. The smell of the earth. The dirt. The fallen leaves. And the taste of blood in her mouth. The ever-present taste of blood, and the saltiness of her chapped lips.

She looked down at Ava. Lying there. Pale. Dirt all over her. Little patches of vomit, crusting at the corners of her lips.

And there were no maternal instincts inside her. She was never maternal. Truth be told, the thought of any kind of responsibility was overwhelming. It ashamed her to admit it, but her greatest urge right now was to get up and walk away. On her own. With no responsibilities. No attachments.

It wouldn't be the first time she'd done that to Ava.

But looking down at her, right now… and then looking around, at the dogs… she could only think of Dad.

The promise she'd made him.

In those final moments, that promise she'd made.

To protect Ava.

To get her out of there and protect her.

That was what she had to do.

She thought about Dad. About how much time they had to make up for. She thought about the conversations they still had to have. And then there was that woman, too. Georgia. The one who had been through all she'd been through. The look in Dad's eyes when he left those apartments. Something had happened to her.

And it hurt her deeply to think... that was just *that*.

You expect life to have neat endings. You expect final cathartic moments. But quite often with life and death, it's just sudden endings. It's words unspoken. It's regrets. Regrets about things said. About things unsaid.

That was the greatest pain of life and death.

She looked down at Ava, and even though she felt fear for where she was, and for whatever was going to come next...

She stroked her hair.

Stroked the hair from her face.

She took a long, deep breath.

She kept on stroking her face.

"You're going to be okay," she said. "I'll look after you. I promise. I promise."

The rain fell heavily.

The thunder rumbled.

And as much as she tried to hold it in, Abigail cried.

CHAPTER THIRTY-THREE

The rain had cleared by the following morning.
And there was more good news, too.
Ava was awake.

Abigail hadn't been intending to fall asleep. Wasn't sure how she could. She just sat up, against that metal fence, shaking. Shivering. She still couldn't understand what had just happened. What she'd just witnessed. Dad. She'd lost her dad. She'd found him again. And then she'd lost him.

And now she was here, with Ava, and with the dogs, trying to understand what came next.

But she must have dozed off. Because she woke to the sound of growling. Rustling. And...

When she opened her eyes, the dog called Doug was right beside Ava. As was the other one. Ghost? Was that what she'd called it?

They were both beside her now. Wagging their tails. The other dogs didn't seem quite as fussed, but seemed curious, anyway.

Because Ava was sitting up.

Awake.

Alive.

And by the looks of things... unaffected by whatever the fuck had happened to her yesterday.

Abigail was still pretty cautious, though. She couldn't *know* that Ava was okay, for sure. Sure, she might be sitting upright. She might *look* okay. But Abigail couldn't know that. Not yet.

One telling thing, though? The dogs seemed okay with her now. Before, they'd seemed unsure of her. Distant. Wary of her, even.

Now... they seemed quite happy being around her.

She looked at Ava, and she felt herself transported back all those months ago, when it was just the two of them, together. It felt like a lifetime ago. She'd tried with her. She really had. But she found it difficult. She'd been tough on her. Really hard on her. Mostly because she was afraid of bonding with her. But also because she was afraid that this kid might end up dying if she wasn't tough enough.

And Abigail couldn't bear that thought.

In the end, walking away seemed like the best option. The best for all.

In hindsight, it was the biggest mistake she'd made in her life.

She thought of Dad. How she'd walked away from him, too. Years ago. For valid reasons. Their relationship. It was strained. She wanted him to get better. To sort himself out. But seeing him depressed, and down, and unwilling to change... that wasn't something she wanted to see.

She'd spent her whole life running away from things she didn't want to see.

She was done doing that.

Ava looked at her. With those wide eyes. Dark circles underneath them, so bold they looked drawn on.

She wanted to ask her about what happened. What she'd experienced. She wanted to know she was okay. For her own sake. And for all their sakes.

She wanted to find out whether what happened at Galloway's place last night was localised, or whether it was more widespread.

She wanted to know so, so much.

But in the end, Ava put it simply.

More simply than she could ever think.

"Brian?" Ava said. Her voice croaky.

A lump swelled in Abigail's throat.

Tears welled up. Stinging her eyes.

As much as she didn't want this kid to see her displaying any weakness… she lowered her head. Shook it.

And she cried.

Ava hugged her.

The dogs came over and cosied up to her, too.

All of them.

All around her.

"It's okay," Ava said. "It'll be okay. Everything'll be okay."

Up above, the sun shone brightly, and the birds began to sing.

CHAPTER THIRTY-FOUR

Abigail walked through the woods with Ava and the dogs beside her, and she wondered where they went from here.

The woods were quite open. The trees weren't thickly compressed together. They were quite sparsely dotted around the place, so the woods felt like they could breathe. There was something calming about these woods. Something familiar about them. She used to go to her woods with Dad when she was a kid. Before everything went to shit. They'd walk down the path, and she'd race him, and he'd always pretend he'd hurt his leg, making her go back to help him before darting off into the distance.

It never got old. It always wound her up. But she always found it hilarious, at the same time.

Dad used to be such a fun guy.

That was the Dad she missed.

And strangely enough... she had lost that Dad a long time ago.

She had grieved for that relationship a long time ago.

Losing Dad yesterday... that hurt. It stung. It was a loss she was never going to be truly able to wrap her head around.

But at the same time, the logical part of her brain told her it was nice that they were able to have those final moments together.

They were able to heal things, even if just for the shortest time.

But the emotional side of her brain...

She felt ruined.

Grief was a funny fucker.

She looked down at Ava. By her side. She was quiet. Pale. Hadn't spoken much since yesterday. Since she'd woken up. They needed to get some food. Some water. Needed to find somewhere safer to rest. Honestly, that's what Abigail was craving more than anything. Rest. Pure rest. She could sleep for days. Weeks. And that's exactly what she intended to do.

She wanted to ask Ava about what she'd seen. What she'd witnessed. When that *thing* was inside her. The thing with the woman's face.

She wanted to know for certain that there wasn't still a trace of that figure inside her.

She wanted to understand why it had burst out of her mouth—her mouth that was torn and chapped at the corners—and yet she was still here.

Still alive.

Not like any other "emergence" she'd seen before.

But Ava was just quiet. And she didn't want to overwhelm her.

She wanted to respect that.

For now.

The dogs seemed okay with her, anyhow. That was a sure sign things were *probably* alright. Right?

She took a deep breath. The fresh, sun-kissed foliage filling her nostrils. A sickly, metallic taste, in her mouth. Ears ringing. The sound of birds the only thing she could hear. Birds were always such a comforting sign. A sign that the infected weren't close.

The blanket of the forest felt like it provided them with an illusory sort of safety. She still wasn't sure whether what happened at Galloway's "safe zone" was limited to there, or more widespread. It felt absurd to assume it wasn't more widespread. An event like the one she'd witnessed. A seemingly *cosmic* event.

That shit couldn't just be restricted to Galloway's.

She found herself thinking of the O.R.I.O.N shit while she walked. The stuff she'd overheard. A project. A project Galloway had uncovered. Unearthed. He was testing on people. Testing on people with this *substance*. Trying to *engineer* the infection, somehow.

An infection that technically wasn't really an infection.

It was more of an...

Occupation.

That's what she was beginning to realise.

She walked down this pathway. What was her goal now? Safety. That's what it came to, wasn't it? Safety. Keeping Ava safe. Staying safe, so that she could keep Ava safe. That was her only goal.

And the dogs, too. They meant a lot to Ava. And they meant a lot to Dad, too, seemingly. She was going to do everything she could to look after them. To protect them.

As terrifying a thought as that was.

She looked down at Ava again, as they walked down this pathway. As the sun peeked in between the trees. As the warm breeze whistled, ever so slightly. The comforting arms of the woods. That's what they needed. That's what they needed right now. Didn't matter what had happened. Didn't matter how the infection—easy to think of it that way still—was changing. Transforming.

All that mattered right now was walking through these woods.

All that mattered was holding Ava's hand.

Keeping her close.

Doing what she could for her.

Protecting her.

She gulped.

She took a deep breath.

She looked over her shoulder.

Then back ahead.

And then she walked down the path, with Ava, and with the dogs.

One step at a time.

She wasn't sure if it was in her head.

But she couldn't shake the feeling that someone was watching.

Closely.

She took another deep breath.

She cleared her throat.

Probably in her head.

Probably.

CHAPTER THIRTY-FIVE

When Timothy Yurin saw the lady, the dogs, and the little girl walking through the woods, he was pretty damned sure he'd seen an angel, right here in his presence.

He sat in his den. Although "den" was probably the wrong word for it, now. It was home. He liked living in the woods. It was nice here. There weren't many people around. Nobody ever came by here. And the evil ones. The ones that tried to hurt him. They stayed away. Far away.

So when he saw these people walking through the woods... he knew he should be afraid.

But he wasn't afraid.

Not when he saw *her*.

When he first saw her, he thought Trudy must have got up and gone wandering. Because she was like her. She was *just* like her. The same shiny hair. The same thin body. The same pale skin. And the same wide eyes.

But... it couldn't be Trudy. Because Trudy was right here. Right here in his arms.

He stroked Trudy's head. Ran his fingers through her hair. So soft. She used to love him putting that nice-smelling melon shampoo in her hair. The one that had a bottle shaped like a pirate. Bath time could be a traumatic event for a child. It was for him. Mum used to hold him down under the water and make him hold his breath. She would smile when he started struggling. And then Dad would always break into the bathroom and drag Mum out and scream at her and—

No. No, Timothy never wanted that for Trudy. He wanted to make sure she was okay at all times. Make sure she was safe at all times. And that's why he didn't want her living with Janet. Because he couldn't trust Janet with her. Because Janet might hurt her. Even though the police told him he had to stay away from her, from Janet, because he wasn't safe to be around children, after what happened with the little boy and the coffin and the spiders...

No. They'd got it wrong. They'd got it all wrong.

So he'd gone in, and he'd taken his Trudy.

And before the police could catch him, before they could catch any of them... the evil ones started walking. Started biting people. Started attacking.

The evil ones were cruel, and they were violent, and Timothy wanted nothing more than to protect Trudy from them. To stop them hurting Trudy.

Because nobody was touching his daughter.

Nobody.

He looked down the slope, as he held on to Trudy. The smell was bad in here, but he didn't notice it so much anymore. It reminded him that he was alive. Really, that's all bad things were, weren't they? Reminders. Reminders that you were still alive. Not always nice. Not always pleasant. But strong reminders of life.

He stroked Trudy's hair a little harder. He noticed that some of it had come away, in his fingers. It worried him a bit. He didn't want to be too heavy-handed with her. He didn't want her losing her hair.

"I'm sorry, dear," he said. "I'm sorry, angel. Here, here's your hair back. Back again."

He watched these people walking by with their dogs, and he found it weird that they were here now. Especially after the weird thing in the sky. The weird noises. He didn't want to look up into the sky when he heard those noises. They reminded him of the noises he heard when the police took him into the Bad Place where they filled him with horrible medicine and made him stop *feeling* stuff.

So he'd hidden in his home. His home made of sticks. And he'd held on to Trudy. He'd told her she was going to be okay. That he was going to look after her. He was going to protect her. He was never going to let anything bad happen to her. Never going to let her come to any harm. Ever.

The sound stopped. And morning arrived fast. He'd got some food for Trudy that morning. A squirrel. A dead one. Left outside their home. Like a gift. Still warm. Still fresh. Didn't smell. Didn't smell a bit.

But now...

He looked at the lady. She reminded him of Janet. And that made him feel sick. He didn't like Janet. Janet wasn't good with Trudy. Just like Mum wasn't good with him.

He looked at the dogs. He didn't like dogs. Dogs scared him. They always growled at him. People used to say it was 'cause he was "bad." But he wasn't bad. He was good. Everyone else was bad.

He looked at the girl, and he saw Trudy in her.

The sister he always wanted for Trudy.

The second daughter he'd always wanted.

He stroked Trudy's hair even more. Even where a clump had fallen away.

"We'll go get you a sister," Timothy said. "We'll save her. Just like we saved you from Mum."

He swore he heard Trudy say "I'd love that, Dad," back to him.

He swore he heard her whisper it.

And that's what he told himself he'd heard.

He watched them walk through the woods.

He waited for them to get just far enough ahead.

And then, when he was sure it was safe, he crept out of their home.

"I'm coming, dear," he muttered. "I'm coming to save you from her..."

CHAPTER THIRTY-SIX

It didn't matter how far Abigail, Ava, and the dogs walked. Abigail just couldn't shake the feeling that someone was watching her.

But those fears soon faded away—*everything* faded away—when she discovered the caves, right in the middle of the woods.

They reminded her of some caves Dad used to take her in when she was little. Although when she was a kid, they seemed so big. So wide. They seemed endless. Mum used to have a go at him for taking her in there. Said they weren't safe. But Abigail used to love the adventure. And Dad enjoyed taking her down there, too.

She would never forget returning to those caves, when she was older. They were far smaller than she remembered. The opening was much narrower. And the most surprising thing was just how shallow they were. There was no depth to them. No depth to them at all.

And there was litter down there, too. Beer cans. Cigarettes. That took some of the illusion of seclusion away. The discovery that those caves weren't these hidden, tucked-away places, in the middle of nowhere. They weren't hers and Dad's special place—their own little discovery. They were somewhere *lots* of people went. Even people who drank beer and smoked cigarettes—and judging by the stray used condom lying around, had sex, apparently.

This cave she was at right now. It reminded her of that cave. Took her right back to her childhood. Because the opening was a lot bigger. And there was a sense of wonder. A sense of wonder surrounding the darkness inside.

Doug went to explore the cave before she had a chance. He didn't seem too fussed about it. Nothing to worry about, clearly. So it must be alright. It was raining pretty heavily, too. The sound of it against the leaves of the forest was nice. Relaxing. Soothing. But they were getting drenched. They were all getting drenched. And besides. It was getting late.

She didn't really want to stop here. Didn't really want to stop *anywhere*, for that matter.

But the weather was shitty. The rain was getting heavier. And she was exhausted, too. Completely fucking exhausted.

She looked at Ava. She'd been good. So good. It took her back to when she was last looking after her. Even then, she had been so good. So strong. She hadn't given her nearly enough credit.

She looked at the dogs, too. They looked happy enough. Running around. The smell of wet dog filling the air. A smell Abigail didn't hate. It reminded her of normality. It reminded her of a world when things were okay. When things were good. When people had no real worries. No real concerns.

She took a deep breath of that wet dog air, as the rain poured down onto her, and as the woods got darker.

And then she let that breath go, with a sigh.

"Come on," she said. "Let's get some shelter."

She walked towards the cave.

Walked towards that dark entrance.

Ava by her side.

The dogs all around her.

As she got closer to it, Abigail didn't notice Wesley—the St Bernard dog—lift his head and look back out towards the woods.

She didn't notice him tilt his head.

Looking right at something.

She didn't even hear his little growl.

Or notice the movement.

In the trees.

Inching closer.

CHAPTER THIRTY-SEVEN

As the sky grew darker, the rain grew heavier, and the wind started to grow stronger, too.

Abigail sat at the entrance to the cave. Ava and the dogs were all behind her. They were all pretty settled. As much as the dogs loved exploring, there was no chance they were leaving this cave tonight.

It was really pitch black. Abigail couldn't even see any light from the moon. Hell, she couldn't even see any trees at this point.

Just pitch black darkness.

She knew Ava was behind her. And the dogs. She'd had a tiny fire lit earlier. But she thought it would be better to put it out when it got dark. Didn't want to draw any attention to their position. These woods were creepy enough as they were.

It didn't help that the wind was really strong, either. So strong that she couldn't hear much beyond it. But in a sense, she was grateful for the lack of total silence. Silence wasn't going to help her racing mind. Her spiralling thoughts.

Thoughts she was trying her best not to lose herself in right now.

She smelled that wet dog filling the cave. It wasn't quite so pleasant now. "Pleasant" probably being the wrong word. *Homely*. Perhaps that was better. A reminder of normal smells. Ordinary smells. The kinds of smells that used to be normal. Commonplace.

But after a while—after the initial comforting tone—the niceness wore off a little. It started to become stinky. Overwhelming. Left a weird taste in her mouth.

She was shivering. Shaking. Really hard. It was easy to forget that she'd only just escaped the captivity of Galloway's place. And while she wasn't exactly in the same sort of captivity Georgia was in, in those final days… it still wasn't exactly the Ritz.

She thought about Georgia, and a knot tightened in her stomach. She didn't know what had happened to her. Not for definite.

But *something* had happened.

Something had happened back there at Galloway's place. In the apartment blocks. When she'd gone searching for those children. Grace's children.

Something had happened there.

She didn't know what. But she could tell from the look in Dad's eyes that he'd seen something he didn't want to see.

She wished she could have done more for Georgia. She wished she could have done more for Dad. She wished she could have done so, so much, for so, so many.

But she hadn't been able to.

There was one thing she had to remember.

One thing she had to bear in mind.

She had done her best.

She had saved Ava. Even when it looked like she was at death's door. She had saved her.

And then she had saved the dogs, too.

All of those dogs.

And they were here, now.

They were all here, now.

She still had that urge. That sudden urge to get out of here. To run away. That need. That need for independence.

Because responsibility.

Responsibility scared her.

Terrified her.

She felt that pull.

Urging her away.

Urging her to walk.

Urging her to leave.

That anxiety.

Building up inside her.

Weighing down on her.

She closed her eyes.

She gulped.

And she turned around and climbed further into the cave, towards Ava and the dogs.

She couldn't see Ava. But she knew where she was. She could hear her breathing, lightly. The dogs snoring right beside her.

She didn't want to wake her up. She didn't want to doze off herself. Not while Ava was asleep. She needed to stay awake. To watch this place.

But she lay down beside Ava and stared up at the darkness.

"I'm sorry about your dad," Ava said.

Her voice filled the silence of the cave.

Cut through the wind and the rain.

A knot in her stomach.

A temptation.

Tempting her to tell Ava to be quiet.

That she didn't want to discuss it.

Didn't want to talk about it.

But...

"Thank you," Abigail said.

Silence.

And then: "He was a good man."

Abigail gulped. Sadness washed over her. That urge, again. That urge to tell her to shush. To stop this. 'Cause it was like peeling a scab off a wound.

And yet…

"Yeah," Abigail said. "He… he was. I just wish…"

She stopped herself.

Ava didn't need this.

But…

"I wish I hadn't pushed him away. I wish I'd had more of a chance to tell him how much he meant to me. How much I loved him. I wish he knew it wasn't because of him that I walked away. It was… it was me. It was all about me. And I feel so bad about that."

She lay there. Eyes welling up. Wind howling. Rain hammering.

And then: "He knew," Ava said.

Abigail looked around to where she was. The way she said those two words. It was with confidence. Not like someone just trying to reassure her. But with a genuine confidence.

Like she really did know.

"When… when you blacked out," Abigail said. But she didn't know what to say after that. Beyond that. She didn't know where she was going with it.

Fortunately, Ava stepped in and finished for her.

"What I saw," Ava said. "It's… it's made me not scared. Anymore. The angry people. And the other ones. It's… it's not scary. It's pretty. So pretty."

And hearing those words… hearing those words made her feel better. About Dad. Because Dad wasn't just dead, was he? He will have been infected. He will have been changed.

And she couldn't even do anything to help with that.

"And he knew. He knew you loved him. He knew you cared. And he loved you so much."

Abigail tried to keep her composure.

She tried to stay in control.

But nothing could stop the sudden array of tears streaming down her cheeks.

She wanted to keep her walls up.

She wanted to maintain that strength.

But right now, at this moment, she couldn't.

She held Ava.

And she cried.

Hard.

And Ava cried, too.

She lay there, as the storm outside grew stronger.

As the wind grew louder.

And as the sound of rain grew heavier and heavier…

CHAPTER THIRTY-EIGHT

Timothy crouched in the darkness and peered over at the caves.
He held Trudy in his arms. She felt really relaxed. But excited, too. He could tell she was excited. She always acted differently when she was excited. Started to twitch. Started to shake her body. Shake her hands and her feet. Like she was happy.

He was pleased she was happy. He was happy too.

Because he was about to get her a sister.

A lovely sister.

He peered into the darkness. Into the rain. He liked the rain. It made him feel calm. Made him feel relaxed. When he was younger, he used to go hide in the shed when it was raining, especially when Mum and Dad were arguing. He'd sit in the shed, and he'd listen to the rain falling on the tin roof, and it would make him feel better. It would make him feel good. It would make him forget everything inside home, even if just for a little while. It would make everything okay.

He could smell her. The girl. Trudy's sister-to-be. She smelled different from Trudy. She smelled of moss and candle wax. He just hoped the dogs were okay with him when he went in there. They would be. He'd find a way to make them feel better. To make them feel comfortable. To make them trust him.

He gulped. His throat was a bit sore. It always got sore, ever since Mum had made him drink the hot water all those years ago.

He'd never forget her pouring the hot water towards his mouth. Telling him that she was going to be okay. Telling him that his mouth was going to be okay. That it wasn't as hot as it looked.

And even though he didn't believe that... even though he thought she had to be lying... he still trusted her.

Because she was his mum.

And she loved him.

Didn't she?

He remembered sipping that water out of the teapot spout. Feeling that hot water filling his mouth, burning it on contact. And Mum smiling at him. Smiling, as she looked into his eyes, as he spat that hot water out.

Then telling him he was a bad boy for spitting it out. For not swallowing it. That he was ungrateful. That children in Africa would do anything for a drink of water, and here he was, spitting it out.

He spat it out. But it made his voice different. Made it really high-pitched. Which made the kids at school even meaner to him.

Which made him want to break their heads and eat their blood even more.

He held Trudy close.

He stroked her hair.

He'd never let her go through anything like that.

He'd always look after her.

He'd always protect her.

Just like he was going to look after her new sister.

He stroked her even more.

For a moment, he imagined her skin was warm.

That she was laughing.

Giggling.

Like she always used to.

And for a moment—for just a moment—he realised her skin was cold.

He had a flash.

A flash of finding her.

A burst of a horrid stench.

And...

Stillness.

He pushed it away.

He pushed it all away.

His racing heart.

That bitter taste.

All of it.

He held her closer to him.

"Come on," he whispered, as the rain pounded down. "Let's go find your sister."

And then he walked towards the darkness of the caves.

CHAPTER THIRTY-NINE

Abigail opened her eyes and her first thought was: *shit. I fell asleep.*

She wasn't sure how she'd dozed off. She'd pledged to stay awake as long as she possibly could. She'd lay beside Ava and the dogs and she'd opened up to that kid. She'd comforted her, too. Comforted her as much as she could.

She'd laid there in the darkness and she had pledged to stay awake. She wasn't tired. Wasn't remotely tired.

But as she knew well, sometimes sleep didn't work quite so linearly.

Sometimes, when she was tired, she found it hard to sleep.

Sometimes, when she wasn't sleepy at all, she'd doze off with the click of a finger.

She should have been aware of that. Should have known better. Shouldn't have let her guard drop.

But even so... what was the worst that could have happened, right?

She didn't really want to answer that question.

She looked up at the dark, mossy roof of the cave. There was a little water gathered on the top of it, dripping down from above.

The ground was really uneven and protruding underneath her back. Digging in deeply. Hell, she wasn't sure how she'd slept a moment. It wasn't anywhere near comfy here.

But again, that didn't mean anything. She'd had the best nights of sleep of her life on friends' sofas. She'd had the worst of her life on a memory foam mattress. The truth was, there really was no rhyme or reason to anything. Not a shred of logic.

She was awake now though. That was what mattered.

She noticed a warmth beside her. On her left side. The same warmth she'd felt when she dozed off. Ava. Had to be. That's how they'd fallen to sleep. And while she didn't exactly feel good about it—she still felt reluctant with any form of connection or closeness, it made her feel deeply uncomfortable—she felt relieved.

Relieved to know she was still there.

To know she was okay.

She took a long, deep breath. She could still smell that wet dog smell in the cave. It didn't bother her quite as much anymore. Initially, she didn't mind it. Then it started to grow too strong. Too overpowering. Then, more bearable again.

There was another smell in the air. An odd smell. A smell she swore she hadn't been able to smell before.

A strange smell of *rot*.

Of *decay*.

Her first thought—gut feeling—was that it was the infected. That they were close. That worried her. Bothered her. 'Course it did.

She lay there and she lifted her head.

Looked out of the cave entrance.

Three of the dogs—Wolf, Buster, Wesley, the last two who seemed to be whining about Dad's disappearance quite a bit, were all sitting around her.

The other dog—Doug—was sitting very still.

Staring out into the distance.

Tilting his head.

Like he was waiting for someone.

Or *something*.

She looked slowly to her side when she realised what that warmth was.

Exactly what it was.

It wasn't what she expected.

It was the dog called Ghost.

He was tucked right up against her.

Curled up.

Whining a little.

When she saw him, dread hit her, right away.

A sudden punch of dread. Right in the middle of her stomach.

Because…

"Ava?" Abigail said.

She sat upright. Bolted upright.

She staggered over to the opening of the cave. She felt energised. Like she'd slept better than she'd slept in years. A long, empty, dreamless sleep. Refreshing. Recharging.

"Ava!" she shouted.

She got to the opening of the cave. Looked outside. Saw trees. Trees, all around her.

But no sign of Ava.

No sign of her around at all.

Logically, she tried to wrap her head around it. She tried to understand it. She must've got up. Gone for a walk. Gone to take a piss or something. She was okay. She was going to come right back here in no time. And when she did, it was going to be okay. Everything was going to be okay.

But there was that other thought in her mind.

That other thought, nagging at her.

What if she didn't come back?

What if she was gone?

She stood there. The dogs around her. In the middle of these woods. The bright blue skies above the trees. The sun shining down on her.

And no matter how much she tried to convince herself that she was okay—that everything was going to be okay, that Ava was going to come wandering back here in no time at all—she knew, deep down, the truth was different.

She stood there. In the bright glow of the light. Fear gripping hold of her. Surrounding her.

And as much as she tried to convince herself otherwise, there was only one reality facing her right now.

Ava was gone.

CHAPTER FORTY

When Ava opened her eyes, she realised right away she definitely wasn't in the cave anymore.

It was weird. She'd had a dream. A dream someone was carrying her through the woods. Her body was so rigid, though. She couldn't move it. It was a bit like when Galloway gave her that stuff, whatever it was. The stuff that stopped her legs working, for a time. It reminded her of that. Only through her whole body instead.

And another thing about that dream?

It felt so real.

But sometimes, dreams did feel real. Especially the ones where she saw the sleep demon. Right at the bottom of her bed. They were the worst dreams. She could never move in those dreams, either.

But when she opened her eyes and realised she wasn't in the cave she'd fallen asleep in, she realised it probably wasn't a dream.

She tried moving her head. But her neck felt really stiff. She could smell something strange in her nose, too. And taste something in her mouth. Like a weird medicine.

She wondered then if maybe that's what had happened.

Someone had given her some weird medicine. Then carried her out of the cave. But then surely that hadn't happened.

Had it?

She looked around the room she was in, and the next thing she noticed was that it wasn't a room at all.

It wasn't a cave, either.

It was a kind of weird hut, made out of big sticks.

It reminded her of a den she'd seen in the woods once. Dad told her a load of kids must've made it. Older kids. He was well impressed by it. Ava was scared by it, though. She imagined a witch, living inside it. A witch who only came out at night, and wanted to chew on her flesh, and crunch on her bones, and turn her body into soup.

Maybe it was because it reminded her of that hut that this place scared her now.

There was something else, too.

Beyond the smell of that weird medicine... she could smell something else.

Something like a mixture of sweat, and...

The worst smell Ava had ever smelled before.

It made her feel sick, right when she smelled it. She could taste it, too. She didn't know what it was. But it was bad. Really bad.

She tried to get up. She didn't know where she was. But it wasn't the cave. The dogs weren't around. Abigail wasn't around. It was dark, and it smelled, and it wasn't nice.

When she sat up, she realised she wasn't alone.

There was a man there.

He was sitting at the door of this den.

He had something in his arms.

Ava couldn't tell what it was. Because the light was really bright.

But this man.

He was sitting by the door.

Long beard.

Long, curly white hair.

And *he* was smelly.

Really smelly.

She could smell his breath.

And he smelled a bit of dog poo. But worse.

And he was looking at her with these yellow eyes where they should be white.

He smiled when she opened her eyes and looked at him. He had these weird little teeth, some of which were yellow, some orange, some black. There were big gaps between them, too.

And just by him smiling, she smelled his breath even worse now.

He looked at her with this smile on his face, and she didn't know what to do.

She didn't know what to think.

That's when he spoke.

"Look, Trudy. We've found you a nice new sister."

And that's when Ava saw what he was holding in his arms.

And when she did…

She felt a whole new level of sick.

CHAPTER FORTY-ONE

Abigail didn't want to give up on finding Ava.
But not even a day had passed, and already she was beginning to lose hope.

There wasn't a trace of her in the woods surrounding the cave. The dogs sniffed around the leaves a fair bit. And Abigail tried to tell herself they were on the scent or something. That they'd found a trace of her, and they were leading Abigail towards her.

But every scent trail always resulted in a dead end. A tree, for one of the dogs to cock its leg at.

There was no trace of Ava at all.

She was nowhere to be seen.

A hard dread took over her. She couldn't stop shivering. Shaking. Not just normal shivers, either. These hard shudders, right the way down her back, all through her body. She felt like she was going to be sick if she walked another step. She kept stopping. Struggling to breathe. Heart pounding. Chest tightening. She'd felt this feeling before. An anxiety attack. Being caught in the grips of panic. It wasn't an unfamiliar feeling for her. She went through a bad bout of it in her late teens. An initial feeling of dread, right in the pit of her stomach. Then the shakes. Struggling to breathe. Heart racing. Sometimes getting dizzy. Sometimes throwing up. A horrid maze that she struggled to get out of, no matter how hard she tried.

She hadn't really done anything particularly special to change things. To "conquer" her anxiety. It'd just kind of... gone away. On its own. Truth be told, she put it down to not having enough to focus on at the time. Of not keeping busy enough. As far as Abigail was concerned, there was a linear correlation between the amount of anxiety a person experiences, and the amount they have to focus on in their lives. It's always the people without much to worry about that anxiety seems to creep up on. While the people with genuine worries—real concerns—were the ones who seemed remarkably adept at surfing their mind's waves.

But right now... that theory didn't quite hold up. She was in a perilous situation. A situation where she'd just lost Dad. And then, hardly any time after at all, and just after letting her inhibitions drop, she'd lost Ava, too.

And now she was alone. She was stranded. With a bunch of dogs. She'd gone from not wanting to be responsible for anyone but herself—because she was afraid of *losing* people—to suddenly jumping head first into responsibility, and having that great fear challenged, almost immediately.

She stumbled through the woods. No sign of anyone. No sign of any infected, or anything. She still wasn't quite sure what had happened at Galloway's place, and how widespread it all was. It seemed like something had *appeared*. Like something had just appeared, in the sky above. And then a bunch of people had vanished. But another bunch of people... they'd broken out of some sort of alternate dimension—that's what it felt like—only in this new infected form, and...

Honestly, she was struggling to make sense of any of it. The thing. The thing that had ripped itself out of Ava's body. The thing with the woman's face.

The thing that had stabbed Dad.

She thought about Dad, and she almost froze again. Griping pains, filling her stomach and her chest. The loss. The pain of his loss. That was never going to go away. Truth be told, she hadn't even processed it yet. Hadn't even *begun* to process it. She wasn't sure where to start. Where to begin.

She didn't have the luxury of being able to wallow in grief right now.

She had someone to find.

But the more she walked, and the more the daylight faded, the more Abigail began to get the sense that her search for Ava was a dead-end.

It felt harsh. Admitting that. She didn't want to admit it. Because that was admitting failure, wasn't it?

But... what else was she supposed to do?

Just keep walking?

Walking, and eventually getting herself into trouble? In deep shit?

But somehow... somehow, self-preservation wasn't quite as appealing anymore. She used to have this strong will to survive. Not to *live*. Just to *survive*. It wasn't logical. It couldn't be. There were plenty of times in her life when she'd wanted to die. But practically, instinctively, her innate survival mechanism had kicked in. Like it always did.

It was frustrating, to a degree. It would be easy if she didn't have that mechanism. She would've died a long time ago.

But it felt like it was the one thing keeping her alive.

That one thread, keeping her going.

And that was another reason she didn't want too much in the way of attachment to anyone.

She didn't *want* any other reason to live, if her survival mechanisms failed her.

She wanted to go.

But then Ava had come into her life. Again. And she'd found this sense of duty. Of responsibility.

A sense of duty that, even though Ava was gone now, didn't seem to be going away.

She stood there, in the woods, and she found herself at a crossroads. A turning point. She had a chance. A chance to just walk away again. A chance to walk away, and go her own way, and go back to her old life. Not a happy life. A pretty damned miserable life. But a far more manageable life than the one she had with someone else involved.

But then...

Ava.

There one moment.

Gone the next.

She wasn't sure why, but she had a gut feeling she hadn't just walked away. Abandoned her. She was pretty sure, somehow, that this wasn't just some revenge mission. Making her pay for her past actions.

She had this horrid gut feeling that Ava had been kidnapped.

Taken.

She wasn't sure whether it was grounded in logic, or in the truth.

But it was a gut feeling she couldn't shake.

And either way...

She breathed in deeply.

She swallowed a lump in her throat.

She knew what she had to do.

There was only one thing she *could* do.

She turned around, and thought about continuing her search, when she saw something, right at her feet.

She walked up to it.

Slowly.

Looked down at it.

Squinted right at it.

It could be a coincidence.

It could just be her seeing signs where there were none.

But as she stood there, as she looked down at this item, the more her heart started to race.

Especially when Doug and Ghost went running up to it, sniffing it, ears tilting, and then wagging their tails.

At her feet, there was a piece of pale blue fabric.

Pale blue fabric that looked just like the shirt Ava had been wearing, when she'd last seen her.

CHAPTER FORTY-TWO

Timothy stared at Trudy's new sister, and he couldn't stop the smile from breaking across his face.

She was lying down on the little sofa bed he'd made out of leaves and twigs. He'd found an old pillow, and even though it had brown marks on it, it was still nice and comfy for her.

She looked so peaceful, lying there. So calm. And even though he'd had to put the smelly medicine over her face that made her fall to sleep, and made her easier to take away, and even though she'd cried a bit, and looked scared now, she was going to be happy here. She was going to be so, so happy here.

And Trudy was going to be so happy to have her as her sister, too.

He stroked Trudy's hair as he stood there in the doorway. It was a shame he hadn't been able to bring the dogs, too. Or maybe just one of the dogs. Maybe the little one. Or maybe one little one and one big one. Then both Trudy and her sister could have a dog each.

That's what he wanted. That would be perfect. The perfect little family.

The sister Trudy deserved.

But also...

He tried not to think of the day he'd found her.

He tried not to think about her eyes.

And then the beetles running across her pale skin.

Or the maggots, or the smell, or...

No.

No, no, no.

He couldn't think of that.

He couldn't think of his failure.

He could only think of getting Trudy a nice new sister, and—

Getting yourself a replacement daughter—

He slapped himself when that thought came into his head. That voice. The voice in his head that said things to him. Bad things to him. The voice in his head that *sounded* like his voice, only it was hard to push away, and sometimes when he *did* push it away, it came back even stronger.

He had to forget those words. Because they weren't true. That wasn't true.

He wasn't getting himself a "replacement daughter."

Because there was no one to replace.

Trudy was his girl. And this new girl. Trudy's sister. She was going to be his girl, too.

No.

They were *both* going to be his girls.

They were both *already* his girls.

He stood there with Trudy in his arms, as he looked down at the wide, beautiful eyes of Trudy's sister.

And as nerves tingled in his tummy... he knew he had to do everything he could to make his new little girl feel welcome, now.

"Hello, princess," he said. "Your name is Rosie. And you call me Dad, now."

CHAPTER FORTY-THREE

Abigail spent two long days searching for Ava before finally finding another trace of her.

It was another piece of her clothing.

This time, a shoe. A grubby, white trainer. Left foot. One of the laces was undone. It bugged Abigail. A loose lace was always a problem. Could trip on it while being chased. Sub-optimal survivalism.

Back in the day, when Ava and her were first brought together, she might have chastised her for it. Told her to be less complacent. She was a snappy bitch back then. It came from a place of care. Really did. But she could have been a bit less heavy-handed with how much she cared. Ava was just a kid, after all.

A kid who now needed her help.

She stood there, in the middle of these dark woods. The sun was getting close to setting. The dogs were all around her. The wind was picking up. It was so silent in these woods. Not even the sound of birds anymore. Which freaked her out.

Just the sound of the dogs.

Snooping around.

Her own heavy breathing.

Shadows in the corners of her eyes.

She focused on the hill above her. The one beyond the trainer she'd found. It looked dark up there. She wasn't mad keen about going up there. There was still this thought inside her. This sense of resistance. A way out. She could turn around. She could walk away. She could leave this place. Right now. She didn't have to do this.

She took a deep breath.

Looked up, further into that darkness.

Beyond the trees.

Into the unknown.

Sure. She didn't *have* to do this.

But she was doing this regardless.

She looked over her shoulder.

Back into the woods.

She couldn't shake the feeling that someone was coming.

That someone was following.

That someone was *watching*.

She gulped.

She swallowed a lump in her throat.

And then she walked up, and into the darkness.

Towards whatever she was about to find.

CHAPTER FORTY-FOUR

Abigail didn't know it yet.
Nobody knew it yet.
Just like, truly, nobody knew what had caused the event. The Threshold Event, as Curtis Galloway once referred to it. Even though he had theories about it, and feelings about what it might have been. He didn't *know*. Nobody *knew*.

But getting back to the point—to the real matter at hand—Abigail didn't know *what* was coming.

In both a metaphorical sense.

And also a very literal sense, too.

She had no idea what was *coming*.

Far away.

Far beyond the woods.

But drawn to her.

Or rather...

Drawn to one *she* was drawn towards.

For reasons she still did not understand.

She walked through the trees, further into the darkness, getting closer to what she hoped to find—even though she did not know that for certain yet, either.

But something was getting closer to her, too.
Something was closing in.
And the closer she got to where she needed to be...
As the dogs started to look back.
And pant.
And whine...
The closer she came to a collision.
A collision with Ava.
With her captor.
But also, with *something* trailing her way.
Through the trees.
In the night.
Getting closer, and closer, and closer...

CHAPTER FORTY-FIVE

When Abigail saw the dark, wooden hut, hidden deep in the woods, she knew right away, deeply, instinctively, that this was the place she was looking for.

It looked like a wooden shack. A den. The kind of den a bunch of kids might make, in the middle of the woods.

And it really *was* in the middle of the woods. Deep in the depths. It might be getting late. But this felt like a part of the woods that the sunlight never reached. It felt cold. It felt like it would always be cold.

It should feel protected from the outside world, somehow. Because it really did feel cut off. Disconnected.

But instead, it felt cursed. It felt unsafe. It felt tainted.

It felt like there was a darkness in this place. An inherent darkness. One that couldn't be broken through. It felt like if the sun ever shone in this place, the darkness would just snuff it out. Like a planet.

Abigail remembered watching this online video once. A simulation of someone falling into Neptune. She used to like Neptune, as a planet. It seemed rather noble and peaceful compared to some of the more chaotic, attention-grabbers like Jupiter or Saturn.

But when she watched this video, she would never forget the realisation that Neptune was so far away from the sun that its light barely reached. That it was further from *Saturn* than Saturn was from the sun. That true, sheer sense of magnitude, really opening her eyes, making her dizzy.

And then the simulation reached the planet's atmosphere, and all light was snuffed out—suffocated—and then Abigail felt truly alone.

She felt like that now, somehow. The dogs were here, with her. But she kind of didn't want to bring them on this mission. It felt unsafe. Them being here. And she felt this need. This need to look after them. To protect them. Almost as if they were an extension of Ava.

She stood there, looking up into this darkness. She saw a little flame. Flickering away inside this cabin.

Cutting through the darkness.

She swallowed a lump in her dry, sore throat.

She took a deep breath.

A deep breath, right into her stomach.

Her exhausted body almost failing her.

Almost.

"I'm here, Ava," she whispered. "I'm here."

And then she climbed the steep, mossy hill, and deeper into the unknown.

CHAPTER FORTY-SIX

Ava lay in the darkness and looked up at the man standing over her, and even though she wanted to run away, she couldn't.

He wasn't a nice-looking man. He had a big bald patch at the front of his head. He had spotty skin. These spots looked really angry. Some of them were red. Some of them were purple. Some of them looked like they'd popped, and this horrid yellow gunk was spilling out of all of them.

She looked up at him and his smile. A lot of his teeth were missing. And the ones that were left were yellow and black. His breath smelled like onions. His whole body smelled weird. The whole wooden den they were in smelled bad. So bad it made Ava want to vomit.

She knew the real reason.

The girl.

The one he called Trudy.

The one he said was his daughter.

Ava didn't want to look at her. Because looking at her might just make her throw up, once and for all. And she didn't want that. If she threw up, the man in here might not like her as much.

And even though she didn't really *want* him to like her... in a way, she did. She needed him to like her.

Because she knew too well already that sometimes, you needed horrible people to like you to keep yourself alive.

She didn't know that he was horrible. He might be nice. He might just be a bit crazy. Mum used to tell her not to be mean to crazy people. To not even call them "crazy people." That "everyone was only one wrong step away from crazy." She didn't know what that meant at the time. She used to think it meant that if she took a bad step, she might fall over and bang her head and it might turn her crazy.

But now, she knew what Mum meant by that. She knew exactly what she meant.

Because she'd seen it in so many people.

She could see it in this man. This man who wanted to call her Rosie.

And she could see it in herself.

She looked up at this man. The smell getting so strong now. There was a candle lit on the other side of the room. Flickering away. Swaying. Her heart beat fast. Really fast. She could feel herself getting afraid. She didn't know what this man was going to do to her.

She found herself hoping that the angry people would come here. That they would come and help her. It was weird. Ever since... ever since *whatever* happened with the *thing* that was inside Mum—the thing that then ripped itself out of her—she almost felt like she had a new sense. A sense that could reach out to the angry people. That could reach out to them and draw them closer. Bring them towards her. Like she was a lighthouse. And the angry people were just following her light.

She lay there as this man stood over her. He was really looking at her. And he kept smiling. Saying things to himself. Things she didn't really understand.

What was weird about this man was that she didn't feel scared by him in the way she was scared of other people. Or other men, anyway. Some men looked at her like they wanted to do really bad things to her. Horrible things to her.

But this man…

The one who wanted her to call him "Dad."

He didn't seem bad in the same way.

He seemed like he wanted to look after her.

Wanted to care for her.

He leaned towards her. He stroked her face with his cold, shaking fingers.

"So long," he said. "For so long. All I've wanted. A sister. For Trudy. A beautiful sister for Trudy."

He smiled. A bit of drool rolled down the corner of his mouth. It was thick, yellow, gooey. It landed right in the middle of her head.

He laughed a bit when it did. Wiped it away. "Sorry," he said. "I… I just want you to know I'm going to protect you. I'm going to look after you. Nothing bad is going to happen to you. I'm going to make sure of it. Okay? I'm going to make sure of it."

He moved down towards her, then. Right beside her.

And when he was beside her… she could see Trudy.

His daughter.

Staring at her.

Silently.

And she smelled so bad—so bad she could even *taste* her—and she made her taste sick in her mouth, and…

The man who wanted her to call him Dad wrapped a thin arm around her. So thin. So bony. So much so it actually hurt a bit.

He pulled her close. But not too close. Just close enough that Trudy was pressing right against her. She could barely breathe.

"We are going to be okay," he said. "Us three. Our little family. Dad. Trudy. And Rosie."

She lay there, her heart beating really fast, as tears built up in her eyes.

"Who am I?" he asked.

She lay there. She didn't want to say it. She felt like Dad would be looking down on her. Watching her. Sad with her, if he knew she was about to say it.

The man pulled her in closer.

So close that she could taste the horribleness of Trudy's skin, now.

"Who am I, Rosie? Say it. Please say it. Please. I just... I just need to hear it. I just need to hear it again. Please."

She lay there. Heart racing. Head spinning. On the verge of throwing up. On the verge of passing out.

"Please say it," the man cried. "Please..."

And she did the only thing she could to make her life just that little bit easier right now.

"Dad," she said.

* * *

AND JUST LIKE THAT, Timothy had everything he needed.

He was home again.

CHAPTER FORTY-SEVEN

Abigail crouched outside the wooden den in the night and tried to comprehend exactly what she was looking at.

But there were some things that just went well and truly beyond rational comprehension, weren't there?

She was right outside this wooden den. It gave her the creeps. Somehow, the woods seemed to get even darker as she got closer to this wooden hut. Partly because it legitimately *was* getting darker. It was night now. Pitch black. She could just about see the moon, peering down from above. But it felt distant. More distant than usual. Further away. Its comforting glow, barely reaching her.

And if there was one thing she needed right now, it was a comforting glow.

She peeked inside this hut. It was hard to comprehend what she was looking at initially. But the more she looked, the more she stared... the more sense it slowly, surely began to make.

The hut itself was actually rather cosy. But it was filled with all sorts of creepy things. Dolls. Dolls that looked broken. Cracked. Toys. So many toys. Crayons. Colouring books.

And right in the middle of the den, someone was lying there.

The first person Abigail noticed was the man.

He was thin. Painfully thin. Had a patchy head that looked like the product of malnutritional alopecia. There were sores all over his body. All over his skin. His face. She swore she could even see little fleas, crawling around his scalp.

He was holding someone.

And that someone Abigail recognised, too.

It was Ava.

She was lying there. Eyes wide open. The candlelight, dimly flickering, illuminating this place with its gentle glow. And Abigail felt this sudden urgency. To storm in there. To grab Ava. To get her the hell out of there. Fast.

But she was frozen.

Frozen by something else.

Right between the man and Ava.

This was the thing that took her a moment to comprehend. To understand.

To really understand what she was looking at.

But when she saw it... when she saw the light flickering against it... suddenly, the stench—and everything else—began to make sense.

Total sense.

It was a corpse.

It could barely even be described as a body at this point. The decomposition was so intense.

It had withered away so much at the head that it didn't even look like it had skin.

But it still had hair.

Long strands of dark hair.

Some of these strands still attached to this skull.

Others...

Others looked like they had been *sellotaped* back on.

To keep them in place.

And it looked the same with the eyes, too.

There was something uncanny about them.

Like they had been glued to the skull, to stop them rolling out.

And this corpse.

It was in a long, blue and white dress.

A little girl's summer dress.

She stood there. Felt a little sick. Her heart started to race. Her stomach started to turn. She needed to get Ava out of there. She needed to keep her cool, and she needed to get Ava out of there.

Because whoever this man was…

He'd kidnapped Ava.

And now she was trapped in there with him.

Trapped in there with this lunatic.

With this psycho.

And—

Suddenly, she heard something.

Behind her.

Movement.

Rustling.

In the trees.

She looked around.

Didn't see anything.

Just the trees.

Just the darkness.

And then she noticed something else.

The dogs. They were all looking around, too.

Looking, with their heads tilted, towards the movement that Abigail swore she had heard.

She looked into the darkness.

Her heart racing even faster.

Her chest tightening.

Her fear building.

Her worry kicking in.

It felt like someone was out there.
It felt like someone was watching her.
It felt like—
Another sound.
Inside the hut.
She turned back around.
Ava was looking up at her.
Wide-eyed.
And Abigail's first instinct was to smile.
To be relieved.
Because Ava was okay.
She was alive.
She was…
And then she noticed something.
The man.
He was gone.
The candlelight flickered out.
Total darkness surrounded her.
And then, out of nowhere at all… Abigail got the distinct sense that someone was there.
In the darkness.
Right in front of her.
Silence for a moment.
Total silence.
Then…
"You dare take my Rosie and my Trudy away."
A high-pitched, broken voice.
The stench of bad breath.
And then, a hard crack in the middle of her face.
Ringing in her ears.
And, silence.

CHAPTER FORTY-EIGHT

Ava saw Abigail appear at the entrance to the den, and she could hardly believe what she was looking at.

She'd come for her. She'd found her. And even though it was dark outside, she swore she could see the eyes of the dogs, too. Glowing in the moonlight.

But just as soon as she'd seen her...

The candlelight had gone out.

And the man who wanted her to call him Dad shot right up, quicker than she thought he'd be able to move.

And then...

Everything went dark.

And she heard a crack.

And then she swore she heard someone falling over.

Hitting the ground.

She lay there in the darkness. She still felt frozen. Frozen, at her legs. Something was stopping her from moving. She wasn't sure what it was. Some sort of medicine he'd given her, or something.

He'd left Trudy next to her. The body, anyway. The horrible, decaying body of the girl he called Trudy. It smelled so bad. And it was covered in little bugs. Earlier in the night, a rat had come in, and nibbled her toes, which were just bones. It was sad. This man. He loved his daughter. He loved his Trudy. And he just wanted someone else so he could be a dad again.

A sister for Trudy.

That's who she was.

But...

Abigail was here.

Abigail was here, and he was going to hurt her.

Unless she did something.

Unless she tried something.

She squinted out into the dark. She could hear the dogs growling. Barking now. All of them. So they were all here. They were *all* here.

And then she heard the man who wanted her to call him Dad speak.

"You dare," he said. "You *dare* come here. Try to take my Trudy away. Try to take my Rosie away. You *dare*."

And Ava could hear coughing.

Coughing and spluttering.

Like he was choking her.

Like he was choking Abigail.

She tried to get up. Tried to get to her knees. Tried to crawl over to him. To stop him.

But she couldn't move.

She couldn't move a muscle.

She heard more coughing.

She heard more gasping.

And then she heard him again.

She could only see a dark mound where he was.

It was dark.

So, so dark.

But she could hear where he was, and see that he was right

over the top of Abigail now.

"I don't want to hurt you," he said. "I don't want to hurt anybody. I never, ever wanted to hurt anybody. But… but you tried taking my daughters away. My girls."

Abigail's coughing was getting louder.

Harder.

"Please—" she gasped.

Ava heard "Dad" crying then.

Sobbing.

"This is your fault," he said. "You made me do it. If you could've just stayed away. If you'd just stayed away, this wouldn't have happened. It wouldn't have had to happen. It wouldn't…"

Ava thought of all the things she could do.

All the things she could try.

Dad.

Calling him Dad.

Maybe that would work.

So she tried it.

She said the word.

"Dad. Don't. Please. Don't."

But it didn't do anything.

It didn't change anything.

She heard Abigail choking even louder.

She looked back around.

At Trudy.

At her dead body.

Which made her feel sick.

So sick.

And she knew now.

She knew what she had to do.

She knew what she had to try.

She looked back around at the dark silhouettes of "Dad" and of Abigail.

She heard the dogs growling.

Barking.

She took a deep breath of that horrible, smelly air.

Then... she did what she had to do.

CHAPTER FORTY-NINE

Abigail lay on the ground, in the darkness, and felt those hard, callused hands wrapping tightly around her neck.

She was flat on her back. This man's hands were tight. So tight. Her ears were ringing. Really loud. She could hear the dogs. Growling a bit. Even barking a bit.

But it didn't seem to be doing anything.

It didn't seem to be changing anything.

It didn't seem to be breaking through.

She just lay there on the ground, with this man on top of her, surrounded by darkness, and she tried to figure out how the hell she was supposed to be getting out of this mess.

She lay there. This man's hands tightening around her throat. She couldn't breathe anymore. Purple lights were flashing in her eyes. Filling her vision. Her ears were ringing louder and louder. She might not be able to breathe properly. But she could definitely smell this guy. He reeked. Reeked of shit. No. *Worse* than shit. He smelled like death itself.

And that made sense. Because of what she'd seen in the middle of this bloke and Ava, just a moment ago.

That girl.

That dead girl.

Lying there.

Right beside this guy.

She stared up at him. Or rather, at the darkness above her. That dark silhouette. She could see the moon behind this guy. Between the trees. It looked nice. It looked bright. It looked bigger than usual, somehow. Staring down at her. Glowing down at her. Smiling at her.

It felt comforting. Seeing the moon up there. She felt like it was reaching out to her. Trying to make her feel better. Trying to help her. Trying to take her away from here.

That's what she needed.

For someone to wrap their arms around her.

To take her away from here.

To...

She thought of Ava, then. Sitting there, inside the wooden hut. In that darkness. She hoped she would run. She hoped she would get up and get away from here and run.

If *she* had to die for her to get away... she never thought she would admit this. But it felt like a worthy trade.

So she lay there. She tried to reach out. She tried to punch this bloke. Or scratch him. Or just do *anything*.

But there was nothing she could do.

Her arms were flimsy.

Her legs were weak.

She couldn't breathe. Not even slightly.

She had that sudden, dark, intense realisation that she was going to die here. She was going to die, on the ground, in front of Ava and the dogs. And that was going to be it. That was going to be the end of her life. Snuffed out, in an instant. Nothing more to it. No greater purpose to it. Just... gone. Just like that.

She lay there and she swore she saw Dad up there, in the darkness. It was strange that it wasn't Mum she thought about. She didn't know what had happened to Mum. She'd tried finding her, after the initial outbreak. With no luck.

But Dad...

She saw him up there, creeping into her consciousness.

Looking down at her.

Smiling.

It's okay. You're almost home. You're almost...

And then, she wasn't sure why, she wasn't sure what was happening, but it stopped.

It all stopped.

She could breathe again.

And she wasn't just breathing. She was coughing. Spluttering. Almost heaving her guts up. On her knees. And the bloke wasn't on top of her anymore. He was...

It was dark. But the moon was shining a little brighter now. So she could see again.

Just enough.

She could see the man. Standing in front of the hut.

Wide-eyed.

And she could see...

Ava was holding the dead girl.

She had a knife to her neck.

Right against it.

And she was looking right at the man.

"Rosie?" he said. "Put... put your sister down now. Put Trudy down now."

"Let us go," Ava said. "And I'll let Trudy go."

The man started to breathe quite heavily. "You—you put her down. Right now."

"Let us go," Ava repeated. Louder this time. She didn't sound scared. Not even slightly.

She sounded... powerful.

And Abigail felt strangely proud of her.

Really proud.

She looked at the man, standing there. Growing more desperate by the second.

She looked at Ava.

Holding the knife to the neck of this dead girl—this "Trudy".

She looked at her, and she knew she needed to do something.

She knew she needed to act.

She knew time was running out.

She was about to step in—to do something—when she heard something.

Something behind her.

Something… approaching.

Footsteps.

She stood there. Ears ringing. A shiver creeping down her spine.

Footsteps.

Definitely footsteps.

And lots of them.

Getting closer, and closer, and…

She looked around.

Over her shoulder.

She heard those footsteps getting louder.

She saw movement in the corners of her eyes.

And then… she heard the worst possible thing of all.

The thing she'd braced herself for.

The absolute last thing she wanted to hear right now.

Shrieking.

Groaning.

And this weird, high-pitched singing.

Getting closer to the hut.

Surrounding them.

They weren't alone anymore.

The infected were here.

CHAPTER FIFTY

Ava held the blade to Trudy's throat, and even though she wanted to get away from here, and even though she didn't like this man—she was scared of this man, the one who wanted her to call him Dad—she couldn't lie, she felt a bit bad for him when she saw the fear in his eyes.

She held Trudy's body close. It was all squelchy, and felt like it was falling apart in her arms. It smelled even worse, too, after moving. So bad that it was making her want to be sick even more. Making her taste sick in her mouth.

She held that blade to her neck.

Saw the man climbing off Abigail.

Then moving towards the door.

Staring at her.

Eyes wide.

"Rosie..." he said. "Your—your sister. Put your sister down."

"Let us go," Ava said. She tried to say the words as strongly as she could. As loud as she could. She wanted him to be scared that she meant it. That she was going to do something to Trudy. She was going to hurt her. If "Dad" didn't let them all go... she was going to hurt her.

"Dad's" eyes looked wide. Tearful. His bottom lip was quivering. His teeth were chattering. He looked sad. Really sad. "You wouldn't," he said. "Your sister. You... you wouldn't."

She looked back at him. And she felt bad. So bad that she was almost tempted to drop the body. To drop it, and then to just run over to him and tell him she was sorry.

Because he wasn't a bad man. And that's what made her feel bad.

Sure, he had kidnapped her. He'd brought her here.

But...

He wasn't a nasty man.

He'd lost his daughter.

He wanted a sister for her.

He needed help.

More than anything, he needed help.

"We can help you," Ava whispered.

The man looked at her. Shaking his head. Crying now. "Please. Rosie. Please."

"You can... you can come with us. And we can help you. We can be together. All of us. But... you need to let us go. And you need to realise. Trudy—"

"Don't say it."

"Trudy's gone."

"No!" the man cried.

It was a horrible cry. A pitiful cry. It was a pained cry. The cry of a father who had lost his child, but still couldn't face up to that fact. Who still couldn't accept that truth.

She looked up into his eyes, as she held on to Trudy's body.

"Trudy's gone," Ava said. "And I don't know who Rosie is—"

"*You* are Rosie."

"I don't know who Rosie is," Ava repeated. "But I am Ava. And... and we can walk away from here. We can all walk away from here. You don't have to be alone. Not anymore."

He looked at her, and she saw him crying even more. She saw

his bottom lip quivering. And she could see the look on his face. In his eyes. Like he knew. Like he knew what she was saying was true, but he didn't want to face it. He didn't want to accept it.

"You can join us," Ava said. "You don't have to be alone. None of us have to..."

She stopped, then. Or maybe she didn't. She wasn't sure.

But she heard something.

Footsteps.

Outside the den.

In the darkness.

And then...

Screaming.

The sound of the angry people.

Or was it the things that came *out* of the angry people?

She wasn't sure.

But whatever it was, they were getting closer.

Closer and closer.

She saw the man turn around, then. Turn around, to the darkness. Like the noise had just about caught his attention.

And then just as suddenly, he looked back around at Ava.

And at Trudy.

And he didn't look as sad anymore.

His cheeks were flushed.

His eyes were red.

He looked...

Angry.

"You aren't my Rosie," he said. "And my Trudy... my Trudy isn't gone."

And then he came towards Ava.

"So you give her to me," he said.

He stepped closer.

"You give her back to me."

Ava pulled Trudy closer.

Pulled the blade closer.

"You give her…"

And then she heard a crack.

A splitting crack.

Cutting through the tension.

She wasn't sure what it was.

Not at first.

She must have closed her eyes for a second.

But when she opened them again…

She saw.

The man who wanted her to call him Dad was lying on the floor in front of her.

He was bleeding from his head.

Crying.

Sobbing.

But he was still crawling towards her.

Or rather, towards Trudy.

Right towards them both.

Abigail was standing behind him.

Holding a hammer.

She looked at Ava.

With wide eyes.

"We need to…" she started.

She didn't finish.

Well. She might have finished.

But Ava didn't hear her.

She didn't hear whatever she said.

All she heard were the dogs, growling.

Then barking.

Then silence.

And then…

All she heard were the screams.

Outside the hut.

Right outside the hut.

In the darkness…

CHAPTER FIFTY-ONE

Abigail looked down at the twitching man, lying in front of her, blood pooling out of his head, and tried to block the approaching screaming and footsteps from her mind.

But that was very hard to do when they seemed to be inching closer every second.

She stepped into this hut. Over the man. She wanted a moment with Ava. She wanted to grab her. Hug her. Hold her close. Tell her how sorry she was for letting her go again. For falling asleep and letting this happen to her.

But there wasn't time for any of that right now.

There was only time to get out of here.

Get away from here.

Hopefully.

She saw the dead girl beside Ava. She saw the sadness in Ava's eyes. The strength it'd taken, to just do what she'd had to do. It was brutal. It was a horrible, horrible world. The things people were made to do. The things *kids* were made to do. It was wrong. So fucking wrong.

And the worst part? Most of the time, you didn't even have

the luxury of time to try to process any of it. To try to wrap your head around it. Understand it.

Most of the time, you were just plunged from one crisis to the next.

That's what it felt like right now.

She grabbed Ava's hand.

And before she could even begin to start trying to reassure her... she pulled her towards the door.

Towards the entrance of this hut.

She saw the shadows.

The dark shadows outside.

She heard the screaming.

Between the trees.

Inching closer and closer.

She heard the dogs.

Growling.

Kicking back.

And in Buster's yappy little case, barking.

She held on to Ava's hand, and she dreaded the thought of running out there.

Into the darkness.

Into the unknown.

Little did she know that Ava had a very different set of concerns right now.

Ava was looking down at the man who wanted her to call him Dad. She was conflicted right now. Which felt like a strange thing to say about someone who had kidnapped her. Who had taken her away from Abigail, and brought her here, and tried to get her to accept a dead girl as her sister.

But Ava looked down at the man and she felt sad for him.

She looked down at him, and she wanted to help him.

Or to comfort him, at least.

She looked down at him, as the screaming got closer, as the

angry people got closer, and the dogs barked louder, and she didn't know what to do.

What to say.

And she didn't know how she was going to get out of here.

How her *or* Abigail were going to get out of here.

She just stood there in the dark, and...

Abigail tightened her grip around Ava's hand again.

Abigail felt frozen.

Frozen with fear.

Even though she knew that was the absolute worst place to be trapped right now—trapped in fear itself—there was nowhere else she could really be.

She stood there with Ava.

She held her hand.

Ava squeezed her hand back.

The dogs all growling.

All standing their ground.

She saw something rustling up ahead, on the left, in the darkness.

Then more movement.

To the right, this time.

She noticed the shrieks had calmed.

They had gone quiet.

They had stopped.

Completely stopped.

But she felt *watched*.

Someone was there.

In the woods.

Peering at her.

She could sense them.

She could *feel* them.

Eyes.

She stood there, and time felt like it was standing still.

She stood there, and she knew she needed to take this opportunity.

She needed to take this chance.

She stood there, and she knew she was going to have to run for it.

Into the darkness.

Into the woods.

With the dogs.

With Ava.

She braced herself to do what she needed to do, when she saw them.

Right in front of her.

Three of them.

Tall.

With jet-black, oily fluid in the place of their skin.

Towering above.

And all with these *faces*.

Human faces.

But something truly, distinctly *inhuman* about them.

They stepped forward.

Into the glow of the moonlight.

They looked at Abigail.

At the dogs.

At Ava.

And then, all three of them opened their mouths, wide, screamed, and scurried towards them.

CHAPTER FIFTY-TWO

Timothy dragged himself across the floor of his home, towards his daughter, his Trudy, and prayed to hold her again.

She was standing now. She was standing, and she was glowing. Glowing with bright white light. Warm light.

And even though he knew it might be something to do with the bump on his head—the one the lady had given him, the one who wanted to take his Rosie away from him, even though she wasn't his Rosie, no, she was something else, she was someone different, nice, but different... he didn't want to think about it too much.

Because he wanted to believe that this was his Trudy.

That his Trudy was back.

She was alive.

He dragged himself further across the floor. His heart beat really fast. There was blood all over the floor. He could taste it, too. Like metal, on his lips. He hoped it wasn't Trudy's blood. He hoped nothing had happened to her.

But when he felt that pain on his head again... he realised it wasn't Trudy's blood at all.

It was his own.

He still kept on pulling himself towards her. Across the floor. The taste of blood getting stronger against his lips. That metallic tang, intensifying. He was crying. But he was happy. He was so happy.

And weirdly, it was because of what that girl had said.

The one he thought was Rosie.

She'd told him Trudy was gone. And it hurt. It hurt, hearing that. It felt like he was being stabbed. Like he was being cut. Really deep.

But at the same time... hearing that girl tell her she was gone.

And then hearing her offer him a chance to leave. With her. With her, and the lady, and all the dogs.

He should have been kinder to her.

He should have been much, much kinder to her.

He dragged himself right over to Trudy. To her warm glow. He could hear things outside. Getting closer. Screaming. And footsteps. And this weird music, too. A weird singing. Like an angel's voice.

When he got to Trudy, when he saw her body lying there on the floor, he cried.

Seeing her, all bony.

All decomposed.

All... gone.

But then he saw that other Trudy.

Right above.

He saw her, brimming with warm light.

He saw her, looking down at him, smiling at him.

And through tear-stained eyes, he smiled back at her.

"We're okay now, love," he said. As the footsteps entered their home.

As the shrieks entered their home.

As the *screaming* entered their home.

"Everything's going to be okay now," he said.

He reached for his daughter's hand.

Her glowing, warm hand.

He pulled her close.

And then the infected swarmed the hut, hurtled on top of him, and sunk their teeth into his skin.

Consumed him.

Tore him to pieces.

Their malleable form seeped into his ears, and his nostrils, and his mouth, and burst through his eyes, and into his skull, and...

Timothy didn't mind.

Timothy just smiled.

He'd felt pain before.

He'd felt pain his whole life.

He was home again.

He was with his Trudy again.

He was...

CHAPTER FIFTY-THREE

Abigail held Ava's hand, tight, and ran as fast as she could through the darkness of the woods.

Away from the infected.

It was pitch black. Truly. The moon, suffocated by the clouds and the trees. They were running on faith. Pure faith. As fast as they could. But nothing was to stop them from slamming into a tree.

Tumbling to the ground.

And if that happened...

It felt like game over.

But what other choice did they have?

What other choice did they have but to run?

She heard the shrieking behind her. It was different from the shrieking of the infected. Those angered snarls. It was more unique. More animalistic. She wasn't entirely sure what had happened to the infected of old. She hadn't seen any since the incident at Galloway's. Since the "event."

It felt like, whatever the infection *was*—whatever the O.R.I.O.N Project had unearthed—the very nature of the infection itself had taken on a second form, now.

A new form.

She could smell a bitterness in the air. A strange scent of rot. Rotten vegetables, specifically. That's what it reminded her of. She could taste it, too. Right at the back of her throat. She wasn't sure if it was something she was imagining, or something real, lingering in the air, making her smell and taste these things. She didn't see much value in lingering on it.

She just held Ava's hand. As tight as she could.

And she ran.

And the dogs ran alongside them.

She wasn't letting go of Ava's hand.

Not now.

Not again.

Not ever.

She wasn't sure how long she'd been running—sprinting—through the darkness of the woods, these shrieks and *melodies* following, unrelenting—when she felt that stitch building in her stomach. When her knees started to buckle. Her body had been through a lot. A shitload of trauma. Relatively recently, too. She'd been living on adrenaline for the last couple of days. Hell, she'd been living on adrenaline a lot longer than that.

And emotionally, too. Mentally.

The things she'd seen.

The things she'd lost.

She bit her lip—hard—and tried to push on through the physical pain, the emotional pain, the mental pain, and keep on going.

She kept Ava in mind.

Firmly in the centre of her mind.

She was the one she was doing it for.

She was the one she was doing it all for.

She pushed on further, the dogs panting beside her, the darkness growing progressively more intense, when she felt something.

Something solid.

Something hard.

At first, she thought it might be a punch. Someone taking a swing at her. Cracking her across the face. Right on the nose.

As she hurtled to the ground, she soon realised it wasn't quite that bad.

But, given the circumstances, it was almost as bad.

Almost.

She tasted the blood.

Felt that stinging, throbbing pain in her nose.

And the crack. She'd heard something crack when she'd collided with...

With what she now realised was a tree.

Ava was still beside her.

Still holding her hand.

The dogs were still surrounding her.

Still all around her.

She looked up at Ava—up to where she knew she was, in that pitch-black darkness, and she said the only word she feasibly *could* say right now.

"Go," she said.

She crouched there on the ground. As the infected inched closer. As their melodies grew louder. Their footsteps... inching closer.

She looked up at Ava, eyes stinging. "Take the dogs. Take the dogs and go."

And she wanted Ava to nod. She wanted her to let go. She wanted her to run.

But instead... Ava did something very different.

Something she didn't expect.

She stepped closer towards Abigail.

Abigail's heart started racing more. "Ava. You have to—"

"I'm not going anywhere," Ava said. "None of us are going anywhere."

Abigail paused. She wasn't sure what to say. What to think.

"I've been looking for home," Ava said. "For so long. For somewhere safe. And now I see it. Now I see. It's here. It's right here."

She looked at Abigail.

She looked around at the dogs.

And as the beautiful, horrifying melodies of the pursuing infected filled the woods... Ava held Abigail, and Abigail hugged her back—hugged her close—and together, together, they cried.

CHAPTER FIFTY-FOUR

Ava held on to Abigail and listened to the horrible sounds getting closer, and weirdly, even though she knew she should be scared, she wasn't scared.

She wasn't scared at all.

She squeezed her eyes shut. It was dark. It was dark anyway. But it was especially dark with her eyes squeezed shut. A few little colours flickered around her vision. Purples, and blues, and yellows. She tried to focus on them. Tried to focus on what shape they were. Exactly what shape. And exactly what colour. Dad once told her to do that, when she was worried about something. Focus on something else, really closely. Like a sound. Or a sight. Or anything.

And when your mind wandered to the horrible thing bothering you again... bring it right back to whatever you were focusing on.

Ava didn't realise she was essentially practicing a form of mindfulness, right from a very young age. A skill that had helped during these times of chaos, especially, in ways she hadn't even fully realised. The ability to shift her focus from her fears... that was useful. Far, far more useful than she even realised.

She could still *hear* the shrieks of the angry people—or whatever they were now—getting closer. She could still *hear* their footsteps. They didn't sound like they used to, though. They were calmer now, weirdly. Like they weren't running so frantically. But they were just heading exactly where they needed to go.

She felt a little bit scared. And the more she noticed that she felt a little bit scared, the more scared she became.

But then she just brought herself right back.

Right back to those colours in her eyes.

Right back to that singing.

Right back to her beating heart.

Right, right back...

Abigail held onto her hand. It was nice. She never thought she was going to see Abigail again after she'd left her. Abandoned her. She was angry with her for so long. So, so long.

But now she was here... she understood. She really understood.

Abigail was just scared, back then.

Scared to lose anyone.

Scared to get too close to anyone.

But she was here, now.

She was here, right now.

She held her hand tighter. Her hand was shaking a bit. She wished she could do something. She wished they could just stand up and run. Run even further.

But Ava wasn't sure how much further she could run.

She wasn't sure how much further she could go.

She'd run so much. She'd run so far.

She wasn't sure there was much more running to be done.

She heard the dogs. Whimpering. Panting. In Buster's case, barking. Yapping away. Even though this was the worst moment of her life in terms of what was about to happen, it didn't feel so bad. She found herself laughing a bit, too. Laughing at Buster. He was such a silly little dog. She hoped he would run away. She didn't want him to stay here. The angry people. They used to be scared of dogs. But the new ones... she wasn't sure if they were the same.

She crouched there and she held Abigail's hand, really tight. And she didn't just feel like she was holding Abigail's hand. She felt like she was holding Mum's hand, too. Mum's hand, and Dad's hand, and Charlie's hand. Charlie, the boy who she'd spent such little time with, but who she was pretty sure she loved, even though she still found the idea of a "boyfriend" rather repulsive.

She held her hand, as the shrieking got closer, as the singing got closer, as the footsteps got closer, and she waited for them to get to her. She wondered what it was going to feel like. Maybe it was because something had happened to her already that she wasn't so scared. She'd already had the thing that came out of Mum's body jump into her. Then break itself out of her. And although it had hurt her mouth, and given her a bit of a sore throat... she hadn't found it bad. She hadn't found it bad at all.

If anything... she had found it comforting.

She crouched there. Right there. As they got closer. As they closed in. As they surrounded them.

She crouched there, and she waited for them to get her.

For them to get them both.

She crouched there, and she waited for the warmth to surround her.

For it to happen.

All over again.

She crouched there, and...

"I'll never leave you again," Abigail said. Squeezing her hand tighter. "I'll never, ever leave you again."

She squeezed her hand back.

Even tighter.

She held her.

Close.

She listened, as the dogs shrieked, and as Buster stopped barking and started whining.

And as much as she didn't want to…

Ava opened her eyes.

She looked around.

And she saw them right away.

The figures.

The dark figures.

Surrounding them.

All around them.

They were here.

It was almost over.

It was almost time.

CHAPTER FIFTY-FIVE

Abigail didn't want to open her eyes and witness what she knew was about to happen.
But sometimes in life, we are powerless to control the decisions our body makes for us, aren't we?

It's like blushing when you're trying not to. You can't help it. You can *understand* the feeling of embarrassment. You can *realise* that it's just a combination of thoughts inside your mind. Irrational self-consciousness.

But, yeah. You *try* stopping yourself from blushing when you're embarrassed. You just try.

And that's what it was like for Abigail, right now.

She opened her eyes.

She looked around, into the darkness.

Tall, dark trees, all surrounding her.

Ava by her side.

Tucked against her chest now.

The dogs.

Forming a ring right around both of them.

And then...

These tall, dark figures.

They barely looked human, standing around them. They looked like the night itself. Some of them weren't the right shape. They seemed... wrong. Something truly *off* about them.

Like there was a *sense* of them having a body, only it was *different* somehow.

Not quite *there*.

She looked at them all, individually.

At these darkened figures.

One, by one, by one.

And what struck Abigail about them was how remarkable it was that they were standing still.

That they weren't moving a muscle.

They were just...

Watching.

Abigail kept looking at them. All of them. She would say she was trying to keep her fear in check, but the chances of that were long gone. The way they stood there. The way they all looked at her. Or *seemed* to be looking at her, anyway. She couldn't see their eyes. But she could sense their gaze. And she knew that soon, there wasn't going to be a thing to *sense* at all.

She wondered what it was going to be like. When they came over here and... did whatever they were trying to do. She wondered if she would feel pain for long. She wondered if she would feel *anything* when they'd found their way inside her body, then burst out of her skin—if that's indeed what they were going to do. She didn't know anymore. She was losing track of the logistics. It was way beyond her understanding.

But she looked at these figures, and then the ring of dogs, and then at Ava, and she tried to focus on what mattered more than anything right now.

Making this girl comfortable, in her final moments.

A bitterness hit her when she thought about that statement. Their final moments. This little girl's final moments. She didn't know what she was seeing. She didn't know what she was witnessing.

But there was no point in fighting it anymore. There was no point in resisting it. She had run. She had run for so long. And in a sense... she would rather fall victim to nature itself—which the infection felt like a part of now—than to any one group or one individual. Dying at the hands of humanity? That fucking sucked. But dying because of a relentless virus that seemed cosmic in origins and wouldn't stop for anything or anyone... yeah, that felt a bit more bearable.

She held her breath. She held Ava's hand. She held her head to her body. To her chest. And she waited.

And waited.

And waited.

"I'm here," Abigail said. "I know I wouldn't be your first fucking choice. But I'm here."

And Ava laughed at that. She actually laughed.

"You're a brave girl."

"So are you," Ava said.

"No. Take the praise. For a second. You are a brave girl."

"Okay. Thank you."

And Abigail laughed at that. Cried, sure. But laughed, too.

And the absurdity of this situation wasn't lost on her.

Crouched here.

In the middle of the woods.

Caked in her own shit.

About to die.

Laughing.

Laughing with a girl she once abandoned.

Surrounded by death itself.

She held her close.

Laughed some more.

Cried some more.

"I told you I'd never leave you," Abigail said.

"And I did too," Ava said.

"Then that makes two of us."

"I just hope the dogs are okay," Ava said.

"They will be."

"You don't know that."

"I don't. You're right. But I like to think they will be."

"I like that you're honest with me," Ava said. "I like that you don't treat me like a kid. And pretend things are good when they're not."

"And I like that you're more grown-up than any other kid I've known. I hate kids."

"Thanks."

And it was magical. Having this conversation. On the brink of death. The best conversation she'd ever had with Ava. Right before the end.

She looked back at the figures.

The dark, silhouetted figures.

Then she noticed something.

One by one.

Slowly.

They started to move.

Towards them.

Towards the dogs.

Towards her.

Towards Ava.

Her heart beat faster.

More sweat fell down her face.

She wanted to close her eyes.

But instead, she forced herself to look.

She was going to look.

She was going to look these fuckers in the eye.

She wasn't going to spend her last moments with her eyes closed.

Ava tightened her hand around hers.

Cuddled her closer.

"I'm here," Abigail said. Putting a hand behind her back. "I'm always here."

She waited for the infected to step closer.

To surround them both.

She watched them inch closer.

Nearer.

She heard their music get louder, as they walked right past the dogs.

As they looked right down at her.

She held her breath.

As they reached their long, dark hands towards her.

Towards Ava.

And then...

As much as she told herself she wouldn't, Abigail closed her eyes.

Darkness.

Singing.

Screeching.

Cold.

And then...

A warm, comforting, peace.

CHAPTER FIFTY-SIX

Abigail opened her eyes.
It was light. Really bright. So bright that she struggled to keep her eyes open. So bright that it actually hurt to stare at the sky.

She was lying down. Lying on her back. On the forest floor. She could see the tall trees on either side of her, shooting out of the ground. She could hear... a ringing. A ringing in her ears.

And panting, too.

The sound of dogs.

Panting.

She squinted. Her head ached. Her throat felt dry. Her body felt... rested. Strangely rested. It was like she was waking up from a long sleep. A long, deep sleep. Refreshed. Renewed.

But still, with that niggling sense in the back of her mind.

That sense that all was not as it seemed.

That something was wrong.

She turned around. Looked to her side. She wasn't quite sure *what* she was expecting to see. But to say she was expecting to see what she saw was probably not entirely true.

The dogs were lying there. All of them.

At first glance, a panic came over her. Were they dead? Had something happened to them when *whatever* happened last night?

But then she saw Doug breathing heavily.

She saw Buster, wagging his back end.

She saw them all, and a newfound relief washed over her.

And then she saw something else.

For a moment—for just a second—this fear.

Ava.

Something had happened to Ava.

Something had...

And then she saw her.

She was sitting there.

Right in the middle of the dogs.

Cross-legged.

Her eyes were wide.

And she was staring up at something.

Up at the sky.

Another momentary dread hit her then. Staring at the sky. Just like the people in Galloway's safe zone had. Just like Galloway *himself* had, before...

Before he fell up, into the sky.

She went to clamber over towards her when she saw something else.

Ava lowered her head.

Looked back at her.

Smiled at her, just a little bit.

Abigail felt confused. Everything seemed... okay. The dogs were here. Ava was here. And she wasn't infected or anything.

She was just... staring at her.

It felt normal.

And that's what felt so wrong about it.

"What happened?" Abigail asked. She wasn't asking Ava directly. More just voicing her thoughts.

A pause.

Then: "They walked away," Ava said.

"They walked away? What…"

She remembered, then.

The darkness.

Fleeing that little den, with Ava.

And those post-infected beings, chasing them both.

Surrounding them both.

Holding Ava.

Bracing for the end.

And then…

"They walked up to us," Ava said. Not looking Abigail directly in the eye anymore. "They… held us. And then everything went funny. And then they just walked away."

Abigail wasn't sure what to say. Her heart beat. Really fast. They'd *walked away*? She didn't understand. Why had they done that? What did any of it mean?

She didn't want to say what she thought. That it was something to do with Ava. Because, so far, Ava was the only one she'd seen one of those creatures surge out of, and live to tell the tale.

Was there something different about her?

And what did it mean?

What did any of it mean?

She sat there on the forest floor. Heart still beating, really fast.

And then she leaned towards Ava, and she hugged her again.

Tight.

She didn't understand what had happened.

How it had happened.

But they were still here.

Somehow, they were still here.

And she couldn't take that for granted.

None of them could.

She held Ava tight, and she felt a little nervous. A little cautious.

Especially when she saw Ghost, the dog.

Glaring over.

At first, Abigail thought it was at her.

But on closer inspection...

He was looking at Ava.

Studying her.

Very closely.

She gulped. And then she pushed that thought—that fear—from the forefront of her consciousness.

Because right now, that didn't matter.

Right now... that didn't matter at all.

"I'll never leave you again," Abigail said.

Ava held her tight.

"I'm sorry. I'll never leave you again. I'll never let you go. Okay? I'll never let you go."

She held her.

Ava held her back.

The dogs surrounding her, in this bright woods.

And even though everything felt so perfect right now—even though everything felt so *good*—there was still that thought.

That sense.

Deep, deep inside.

That sense that something was wrong.

That she wasn't going to be able to keep that promise.

She gulped again.

Gulped down that sickly lump in her throat.

She might not be able to keep it.

And something *might* be wrong.

But she was going to try.

She was going to damned well try.

CHAPTER FIFTY-SEVEN

Abigail stood at the edge of the woods with Ava and looked up at the sky.

It was blue. Really blue. Almost too blue. There wasn't a cloud in sight. It looked almost perfect. There was something unsettling about it. It was the same as the morning she'd woken up at Galloway's place. After the "event." Reminded her of that.

But she was doing her best not to read too much into things right now.

She was doing her best just to take things at face value.

And face value was clear right now.

Ava was beside her. Looking up at the sky, too. But it felt like she was looking *at* something specific up there. Like her eyes were focused on something. Settled on something.

Something Abigail couldn't see.

"You okay?" Abigail asked.

Ava looked around at her. Nodded. "Yes."

She wanted to ask her if she was sure. It wasn't in her nature. Being a mother hen. But it had taken over her, to an extent. This urge. This primal urge to look after her. To protect her.

She looked down at the ground, then. At the crosses. The ones they'd placed. For Ava's mum. And from Abigail's perspective, for Dad.

There were so many more crosses she could lay. So many more people she could lay them for. So many memories of people she'd lost.

But right now... she looked at this cross, and she saw Dad there.

She saw him, standing there.

In the chaos of Galloway's safe haven.

Eyes focused on her.

Sadness in his eyes.

But also happiness, too.

Pride.

She found herself lost in this memory. If it even *was* a memory. Wanting to tell Dad she was proud of him, too. That she loved him. And that she was going to do everything she could to continue to make him proud.

To continue his legacy.

She looked at Ava.

She looked at the dogs.

Then, she looked into the distance.

Towards whatever lay ahead, on this road ahead.

"Come on," Abigail said. "Let's go."

"The sky," Ava said.

Abigail looked up.

At that perfect blue.

Then back down at Ava.

Eyes still fixed on the sky.

"What about it?"

Ava looked at her.

Her eyes wide.

She opened her mouth.

Like she wanted to ask Abigail something.

Then she just closed it.
Shook her head.
"Nothing."
"Are you sure?" Abigail asked.
Ava nodded.
Abigail wanted to push.
She wanted to push for more.
Because Ava had seen something.
There was no doubt about that.
Ava could see something that she couldn't.
But before she had a chance… the moment was gone.
Ava started walking.
The dogs started walking.
Abigail took a deep breath.
She swallowed a lump in her throat.
She looked at that cross again.
Those two crosses.
"I'll do you proud," Abigail said.
And then, with the dogs by her side, and Ava by her side… she walked.

* * *

Ava looked up at the sky and wondered whether what she was seeing was in her head or not.

It seemed like it might be. Because Abigail didn't seem to be able to see it.

But every now and then, when the things moved, she thought she saw the dogs looking up, too.

Like they could see it, too.

"Come on," Abigail said. "Let's go."

Ava looked at Abigail.

Her face looked worried. Pale. She loved Abigail. Even though she'd left her before. And that had hurt her. She loved her.

She wanted to ask her. About the sky. Whether or not she saw anything.

But she didn't want to worry her, either.

"The sky," she said.

She stopped herself, then. Just saying the words. It seemed to make the things in the sky move.

"What about it?" Abigail asked.

Ava's tummy turned. Her heart beat faster. Harder. She looked back up at the sky. Past Abigail. At that *thing*.

She wanted to tell her.

She wanted to tell her everything.

Instead...

"Nothing," Ava said.

She looked at the ground. At the dogs. They looked like they were looking at her. Then looking up, too.

Like they knew her secret.

"Are you sure?" Abigail asked.

This was it. The last chance. The last chance to tell her what she saw. The last chance to tell her the truth.

But instead...

She gulped.

She looked at Abigail.

She nodded.

Abigail looked like she wanted to keep asking her what she saw.

Like she didn't believe her.

But then she just smiled back at her.

And before she could ask anything... Ava started walking.

She waited for Abigail to say something.

She almost *wanted* her to ask her, again.

But instead... as she walked away, it wasn't long before she heard Abigail's footsteps, following, right behind her.

She walked into the distance.

Into the unknown.

She tried not to think about the night before.

To think about what had happened.

And to think about the truth of what happened when *they* surrounded her, Abigail, and the dogs in the woods.

She'd told Abigail they'd just walked away.

She knew that wasn't true.

But she tried not to think about it.

About any of it.

And she tried her best not to look up at the sky.

At the big, black things, floating through it.

Those long, stringy, black tentacles, dangling down from underneath them.

And the bodies.

Human bodies.

Dangling down from those strings.

Everywhere.

END OF BOOK 8

Pandemic Z 9: New Dawn, the ninth book in the Pandemic Z series, is now available.

If you want to be notified when Ryan Casey's next novel is released—and receive an exclusive post apocalyptic novel totally free—sign up for the author newsletter: ryancaseybooks.com/fanclub

Printed in Great Britain
by Amazon